GEORGE MORENO JR

Cursing The Moon

Lunar Psycho

MORENO VENTURES PUBLICATIONS

First edition

ISBN: 9798985385311

This book was professionally typeset on Reedsy.
Find out more at reedsy.com

As a child I grew up fascinated with werewolves. I carried that fascination with me through my adolescence into adulthood. I have been able to share my love of Sci-Fi and werewolves with my wife and two children, and now I am finally able to put it all together and share the experience of writing this novel with the people I love most in this world. This novel is dedicated to my family.

Contents

Acknowledgement

Thank you to my wonderful wife for pushing me to follow my dreams and put my vision onto paper and bring it to life. I am truly blessed to have you in my life.

Thank you to my children for giving my honest feedback and constructive criticism throughout the long process of writing this novel. You two are the greatest gift that I was ever given, and I am proud of the people you are becoming.

Thank you, Amanda Armstrong and Publify for giving me the tools and resources that I needed to put my book on the market. The Publify group was instrumental in helping me bring everything together.

Thank you to all of the incredibly talented people that helped me edit, proofread, design, and illustrate my novel. I am extremely proud to have you on my team and I love that your hard work is also on display with this novel.

Thank you to Jennie Lyne Hiott at bookcoverit.com, for the beautiful artwork and design of my book cover.

Thank you to Paul Kent Sewell for the amazing illustrations and bringing my visions to life.

Thank you to Mallory (Penofadventure via Fiverr), for your proofreading, editing, and helpful suggestions.

CHAPTER ONE: SLAUGHTER CREEK

Dusk was upon the great state of Texas. There was enough sunlight left to illuminate the roadway and brilliantly define the multitude of colors that the landscape of the IH-35 had to offer. A 2012 black Chevy pickup truck was barreling down the highway from San Antonio when the bump of a tire rolling over a wood plank at eighty-five miles per hour lifted the vehicle occupants off their seats.

"Whoops!" George uttered with a laugh.

"Whoops? Whoops?! What do you mean whoops, George?!" D yelled at her brother. "Dad will kill you if something happens to his truck!"

"Geez, I know, sis! I know! Chill. The truck is fine and so are we!" George snapped back.

"You two fight over everything. I love it, it's hilarious!" Austyn said as he added his voice the siblings' spat.

"Shut up, Austyn! You and my brother are idiots!" D retorted, and she plugged her headphones into her ears, letting her music drown out the two men in the vehicle with her.

George and Austyn looked at each other and shrugged simultaneously and laughed.

The three young adults had all graduated from St. Francis College Prep Catholic High School. George and Austyn were both nineteen years old and D was about to turn twenty-three. The trio was en route to Slaughter Creek, a small suburb just south of Austin. It was October 30th and a Friday, a great night to go to one of the scariest haunted houses in Texas, according to "PLEY". PLEY was a social media platform used to give reviews on just about anything. This was the first time George had been given permission from his dad to use the truck to go out of town, and while he was excited, he knew that he was given permission only because D was going along too.

As time neared the seven o'clock hour, the sun was setting in the western horizon of the Texas skyline. The warmth and vibrant colors emanating from the rays of sunlight were slowly giving way to the colder gray tones of the night sky. The roaring of the pickup was waning as the trio of thrill seekers pulled into the parking lot of what was known as "Slaughter Creek's House of Terror".

"Hell yeah! We're here!" George exclaimed enthusiastically.

"Gotta hand it to' ya, little man, you got us here alive," D remarked.

George acknowledged her words with a nod and a smile, shut the engine off, and retracted the key from the ignition. Austyn excitedly slugged George on his upper arm and hopped out of the truck with a howl. George climbed out of the truck and returned the arm slug to Austyn, calling him an *"ass"* for good measure.

"Y'all are both idiots," D commented as she stared at the two tussling young men and waited for them to catch up to her.

The two friends could easily be mistaken as brothers. They were similar in height, weight, build, and hair color. They even shared a sense of humor and style. George, with his short-cropped black hair and brown eyes, stood six feet, two inches tall, and was lean and athletic. Austyn stood six feet, one inch tall, had a muscular build, and dark brown hair, and brown eyes.

D— short for "Damaris" —on the other hand, was quite the opposite of her brother and his friend. She stood five feet, three inches tall, had an athletic build, light skin, shoulder-length dark brown hair, and brown eyes.

George and Austyn caught up to D and the three walked to the entry booth that was stationed on the right side of the entrance gate to the dark and gloomy building. The group joined the line, noting four groups ahead of them.

"Forty-five bucks per person?!" griped George when he saw the single participant entry fee. "Austy, if this place sucks, you're walking home!"

2

George added, glancing at Austyn. Austyn responded with a simple shoulder shrug and smirk.

"This is gonna be fun! My friends Celia and Zee said it will scare the crap out of us!" explained D excitedly.

George faced forward and stepped up to the window to begrudgingly pay for his pass. George hated parting ways with money. From the time he was a child, he would take all of the money that he received as birthday or Christmas presents, and any loose change he could find (including taking all the loose change his dad had in his wallet), and put it all into his piggy bank, shaped like a baseball glove and ball. He knew exactly how much money he had in there and would boast to his sister about how much money he had saved. Whenever the occasion arose where he needed to dig into the bank and take money out, he was sure to put whatever change he had left right back in.

George peered through the plexiglass window and saw the expression of utter boredom on booth worker's face. His body language indicated that this small both, on the night before Halloween, was the last place he wanted to be. The "Slaughter Creek's House of Terror" t-shirt he was wearing was badly wrinkled and appeared as if it was taken off at the end of every shift and left crumbled up until he needed it again. He was also wearing a lanyard with a monster themed name tag that read *"Screamin' Steven"*.

"Just for you?" Steven asked George.

"Yeah, these losers are on their own," George answered, motioning his thumb over his shoulder to where Austyn and D were standing behind him.

"That'll be $48.71, after taxes," Steven said.

"Damn near fifty dollars for this!? And I still need to pay for food and gas!" George lamented loudly. He was about to go on another mini-rant but stopped himself when he remembered that there was still a line behind him, not to mention "Screamin' Steven" didn't look amused. George reached into his wallet and slid his money under the plexiglass.

"This better be worth it," George mumbled one last time, awaiting his change.

"One dollar and twenty-nine cents is your change," Steven replied and slid the change back to George.

D and Austyn paid their fees with much less of a fuss than George and all three moved onto the next line that led to the haunted house entrance.

Unlike most haunted houses that are set up in an abandoned warehouse or multi-level commercial buildings, Slaughter Creek's House of Terror was a real house. Though, with its size, it was more akin to a mansion than a house. One of the appeals of this particular haunted house was knowing that they were in a home that was once lived in. This three-story monolithic building was well taken care of, but its age and the elemental wear were clearly visible.

The anxious crowd of all ages looking for a good scare and a good time were filed in line leading up to the patio aligned with torch-like fixtures. The uniqueness and lure of the attraction drew crowds from all around, but only forty people were allowed to enter at any one time.

Mixed in the middle of the growing line was the triad from San Antonio. They were laughing and passing the time with jokes and making bets on who would be the first to get scared. For Austyn, thoughts of D being frightened and clinging to his arm raced through his mind. He had never really thought of D as anything more than his best friend's older sister, but as they got older, he noticed how beautiful she was and began to develop a crush on her. He thought she was gorgeous, funny, tough, sarcastic, and intelligent; all traits that he absolutely adored. He had not yet told George how he felt about D, because he didn't want to make things weird.

Wow, she smells good, Austyn thought as the scent of D's expensive perfume filled his nostrils. Austyn did his best to not let his true feelings show on his face as D continued to talk about the time she thought she saw a ghost at her grandparents' house. All Austyn could do was smile, listen, and think, *One day I'll tell you.*

George was feeling anxious. He was always one to get excited about things and he could not wait to see if all of the hype was true about this haunted house. *Hurry and let us in, so I don't have to listen to my sister's boring ghost story for the millionth time,* he thought to himself.

"Oh look, the line's moving! We're almost next!" D said, growing more excited.

D was a bit of an adventurer and thrill seeker who often fell victim to a good jump-scare. Leading up to tonight, she had told George that she had only come along because their dad had asked her, but, truth be told, she had been wanting to see Slaughter Creek's House of Terror ever since her friends told her about it.

As they waited in line, D looked at her brother and smiled. She loved her brother, but he was very good at annoying her. She took pride in not letting things get under her skin, but George seemed to have a talent to do just that, and in turn drive D crazy.

Up and down the exterior corridor, screams, growls, and howls could be heard coming from within the walls of the house. Some of the sounds were sound effects, but most were from the visiting patrons that were already inside the House of Terror. Employees dressed in monster garb continuously trolled the line looking for a weak link to scare and send the crowd into a frenzy. During the ruckus, a demon-type monster snuck up behind a group of girls roughly the same age as George and Austyn. The demon hissed into one of the girls ears and she instantly screamed and turned, running right into George. She gripped him tight and buried her face into his chest.

George stood open-armed and happily surprised that an attractive girl was clutching onto him. The short blonde haired, blue-eyed girl looked up at a smiling George and asked, "Is he gone?"

"Yes. He's gone," George replied. He and the scared girl watched as the demon continued harassing people down the corridor. After regaining her composure, she realized what had just happened and with an embarrassed tone and a flushed face noticeable even in the dark, the girl uttered, "I'm so sorry about that."

"No worries. I'm here anytime you need me. I'm George, by the way." The words had escaped George's lips before the euphoria of the moment had passed and allowed him to properly process and filter his response.

"Hi George, I'm Emily," she replied with a smile and extended her right hand to George. He reached out and shook Emily's hand, much to the shock of D and Austyn, who were staring at him like they had no idea who he was. It was out of character for George to be so brazen, and even more out of character for him to be smooth.

"NEXT! It is your turn to step inside the doorway of eternal terror and torture. MmmWahahaha!" declared an employee dressed in a full grim reaper costume. He bowed and motioned with his left arm as if to guide the next group into the house.

"I guess we're next," Emily said to George.

"Have fun. Be safe," George replied with googly eyes and a grin. Emily smiled back then turned and took a step forward to join her friends, but she suddenly stopped, turned, and rushed to George.

"Can I see your phone?" Emily hastily asked George with her hand out.

"Uh, uh, sure, here." George was caught off guard by the request and instead of denying handing his phone over to a complete stranger, he struggled to pull his phone from his pant pocket. George finally found the phone and handed it to Emily. She quickly typed something and then returned it.

"My number is there, I just sent myself a text message. Bye!" Emily exclaimed and raced back to her friends.

George stared at his phone and looked up in time to see Emily looking back at him before she disappeared into the darkness of the house.

"That was awesome!" George celebrated with a fist pump.

"Nice!" Austyn joined in with a high-five for his best friend.

D contemplated making a snide remark, but she decided to let her little brother bask in his newfound glory. She liked seeing her brother happy; besides, she still had an hour's worth of drive back to San Antonio to roast him. D was about to comment on how random the whole event had been when suddenly the loud, creepy voice was ushering them into the house.

"George! Now you can follow your little girlfriend Emily into the darkness and to your demise! MmmWahahaha!" announced the grim reaper. The group of three looked at each other and laughed before they stepped inside the "House of Terror".

Once inside they walked through a misty cloud. When the fog cleared, a young man jumped out in front of the group and shouted "STOP!"

As predicted, D screamed and jumped back. Austyn and George laughed and quickly turned their attention to the character who appeared to be dressed as a tomb raider.

"A warning, before you venture any further! You should turn back now while you still can, there are cursed and terrible things of a supernatural origin ahead! If you dare to defy my warning and proceed, then take these, and hopefully you'll find your way out of this nightmare!" The tomb raider extended his right hand which held a green, an orange, and a blue glow stick.

D grabbed the glowsticks out of the raider's hand and gave the orange stick to George and the green stick to Austyn, keeping the blue one for herself.

"Good luck, you fools!" The raider added and disappeared once again into the fog.

"Sis, he wasn't even a monster and you still got scared!" George laughed at his sister.

"Remember, they can't touch us!" Austyn reminded D in an attempt to be helpful.

"I know that, Austyn! Let's move, people are waiting," D responded sneering

7

at the two of them.

George raised his left arm with the glow stick and led the way into the next room. Screams echoed from all directions, temperatures changed from chilly to near freezing, and glowing red and yellow eyes surrounded them.

Forty-two bone chilling minutes later, the trio emerged from the exit at the rear of the house. Being pursued by four maniac clowns with instruments of malice, they pushed through the doorway and out into the open.

"It's over, Pennywise! Take your clown car crew and get out of here!" George shouted at the slowly retreating clowns.

"Woohoo! That was awesome!" Austyn said, side hugging D happily.

"We have to do this again next year! They say that the layout changes every year!" D explained to the guys.

"I agree; it was worth the $50 bucks I just shelled out! *And,* since D was scared first, she has to pay for our food!" George crowed, celebrating a personal victory.

The haunted house did not disappoint. The group had never experienced an atmosphere quite like it. The trio talked and laughed while walking back to the truck. As they walked, George felt his phone buzz. He reached into his pocket and retrieved it to see what the notification was.

"Who is it? Everyone that you know is here with you," D said, joking with her brother.

"It's from Emily!" George's eyes gleamed with happiness as he read the text message.

"Well, what does it say?" Austyn asked eagerly.

"She said that her and her friends are going to the creek. It's a hangout that the locals visit and she invited us to go if we want," George explained to D and Austyn.

"I'm game!" Austyn responded and raised his hand.

"Oh George, I don't know. I'm sure dad wants his truck back at a decent time. Maybe we should just go home," D said.

"Of course, you would say that. You never want me to have my way! I never ask you for anything D, the least you could do is let me have this!" George lamented to his sister.

D stared at her brother in amazement. For a split-second, she thought of ways that she could physically beat her brother, but then she began to consider her brother's feelings and the fact that he would definitely support her if she were in the same situation.

"Okay, George, we can go for a little while. It's been a fun night and I just want to get home safe," D relented.

"I love you, sis! It'll only be for a little while! Thank you!" George jumped and squeezed his sister tightly. He quickly responded to Emily's text message letting her know that they were in and asked for directions to the creek.

D smiled and looked at Austyn, who was staring back at her with a warm smile.

"What?" D asked curiously.

"Oh…uh…nothing, just thinking," Austyn said, stumbling over his words after she caught him staring at her in a daze.

"Weirdo," D responded and directed her attention to her very happy brother who was eagerly awaiting a response from Emily.

George's phone received the text notification. He read through the message and looked around the area that they were parked.

D and Austyn looked at him, puzzled, and asked, "What are you looking for?"

"What section of this lot are we in? Emily said they are still in the parking lot and they will come to us so we can follow them to the creek," George told them.

"Look there, we are in the "Witch" section!" Austyn informed George as he pointed directly behind him to a light pole with a logo of a witch. George sent a text message to Emily letting her know that his black Chevy pickup was parked in the "Witch" section. He stared at his phone willing Emily's response to appear immediately. A moment later, he received her response and lifted his head to scan the large parking lot. He let D and Austyn know that she was on her way to be on the lookout for a small gray SUV.

D saw headlights turn the corner at the north end of the aisle and pointed. "I think that might be them."

A gray SUV with Emily sitting in the passenger seat and three other girls sitting in the backseat pulled up next to the trio.

"Hi guys!" Emily greeted the three.

D and Austyn acknowledged with a hand wave. Introductions were made between the two groups, and it turned out that Emily was from San Antonio as well. She was visiting her cousin who was a college student at the University of Texas. Quite the happy coincidence, as far as George was concerned. He was chatting it up with Emily and learned that she was a high school senior at North San Antonio High School. After a few minutes of chit-chat, George, D, and Austyn jumped into the truck and both vehicles exited the parking lot, George following Emily's cousin Sarah closely.

"Remember, only for a little while, George," D reminded him. "It is getting kinda late . We waited in line for a while and then took almost an hour to get through the haunted house."

"Yes, yes, yes, only for a little while," George responded, annoyed by his sister's reminder.

"Relax, D. We both know that something like this will probably never happen to your brother again. Besides, we will stick together and keep each other company," Austyn added optimistically .

"I guess, Austyn, but there are supposed be more people out there and I'm sure you'll ditch me for one of those girls that is riding with *"Emaaaaalyyyyy,"* D said, sharing her thoughts in a childish tone, mocking Emily's name in an attempt to get a rise out of George.

"And *I'm* the immature one?" George mumbled sarcastically under his breath.

After a good ten-minute drive, the vehicles finally entered a clearing that served as a makeshift parking lot. There were already several cars parked and music could be heard blaring from beyond the tree line. The SUV and the truck pulled into to the lot and parked. The group in Sarah's vehicle climbed out and made their way to what appeared be a trailhead that led into the wooded area. Emily stopped at the entrance and turned to wait for George, D, and Austyn who were just dismounting the truck.

"C'mon guys! The creek is just a little further!" Emily said, waving her right arm like she was a third base coach waving home the runner.

"Yeah, c'mon!" George prompted D and Austyn, increasing his pace.

D rolled her eyes behind her brother's back and Austyn nudged her with his elbow, encouraging her to keep moving. Austyn was all for seeing his buddy get lucky with a girl.

When they were on the St. Francis Varsity baseball team, Austyn, the second baseman, and George, the shortstop, worked well together, always coming through for one another on plays. The duo had been dubbed *six-four-three* by their coach; a common term used for the success of a middle infield double play. Austyn saw the current situation as no different than when they made double plays on the baseball field. He was ready to back up his teammate any way he could.

Austyn was also anticipating spending some quality one-on-one time with D while George was distracted with Emily. *This is what I need, a window. Have to start a good conversation with her and get her laughing. If I can get her to laugh it will make things less awkward*, Austyn thought to himself.

Emily was leading the small group of four, with George by her side, down the trail. Thankfully, the glowstick that George kept in his pocket from the Slaughter Creek House of Terror, was still glowing brightly and it, along with Emily's cell phone, helped illuminate the dark path. The music grew louder and so did the sound of laughter and chatter.

There was an opening ahead to an area near the water that was lit brightly by the now full moon hanging directly over the creek. The group reached the opening and emerged into an almost club-like atmosphere.

By D's count there were close to fifty people dancing and having a good time. *This doesn't look that bad"*, D thought to herself. She and Austyn gave George some space to be alone with Emily, and they headed closer to the creek. D marveled at the crystal-like quality of the water. The moon looked brilliant, and it brought about a sense of calm and security.

"What do you think about this place?" Austyn asked D in an attempt at starting a conversation.

"It seems okay, no one looks psychotic or anything," D replied, looking around at the crowd.

"For sure," Austyn agreed almost absentmindedly. "But hey, don't worry; if anyone *is* psychotic, I won't let anything happen to you," he told her, receiving a puzzled look.

"Oooookay!" she uttered with a sideways look at Austyn.

"Uh, I mean...you know...being that you are my best friend's sister," Austyn stammered, attempting to backtrack .

"I guess," she frowned at him. "But it's fine; I can take care of myself. Ask your buddy how many times I've made him cry," D replied boastfully.

There was a brief moment of silence and then they both laughed. As the night wore on, the conversation was going well, despite a shaky start. Austyn had accomplished one thing that he had set out to do: make D laugh.

George, some distance away, momentarily turned his attention from his own conversation with Emily to see Austyn and D getting along very well. He was surprised by this but shook his head and turned his attention back to Emily.

"Yeah, we graduated last year. He is like a brother to me; he knows my secrets and I know his," George told Emily, explaining the dynamic of his friendship with Austyn. George often used the term "bruh" when talking to friends and acquaintances that were guys, but with Austyn he always used "bro" because he felt that Austyn was his brother. He even believed that forces of nature had forged their friendship because they had both attended the same school since kindergarten. George's last name was Bala, which was Spanish for bullet, and Austyn's last name was Silver, making the duo a Silver-Bullet.

They grew up a few houses away from each other and spent almost all of their time together. One day, the two had watched *"Blood Brothers,"* a movie about two best friends that became blood brothers by drawing blood on their palms and shaking hands. Immediately after seeing this, George and Austyn found a piece of broken glass and used it to cut their own palms, pledging to be blood brothers.

After George finished his story about Austyn's and his friendship, Emily told him that her cousin's friend thought Austyn was cute and wanted to know his current dating situation.

"Is he single?" Emily asked George.

"Yes, as a matter of fact he is," George answered happily.

"Do you think you can ask him to maybe go and talk to her?" Emily requested.

"Sure, why not!" George replied. He motioned for Emily to stay where she was and he walked over to where D and Austyn were talking.

"Hey!" George interrupted their conversation.

"What's up?" Austyn asked.

"I need to talk to you," George said urgently, nodding at Austyn.

"George, it is past ten already, are you almost done?" D interjected.

"Again sis, really? Give me an hour, that is all I'm asking," George pleaded. "We will be on the road by eleven."

"Fine, but if you aren't ready to go by then, I'm going to embarrass you in front of Emily, take the keys, and drive home. With or without you!" D said forcefully.

"Okay!" George snapped. Then, motioning for Austyn to follow him he said, "Austyn, over here!"

Austyn's heartrate was accelerated; he was sweating and had cotton mouth. He was sure that George was going to question him about what he was doing with Damaris. When the two came to a stop Austyn immediately started trying to explain what he and D were doing, but George hushed him.

"Shut up and listen bro. Emily's cousin Sarah has a friend that thinks you're cute," George said excitedly.

"What?" Austyn was completely blindsided by George's words.

The look of perplexation on Austyn's face made George laugh and he gave Austyn a shove.

"I know! I can't believe that anyone thinks you're cute either," George joked with his friend.

"Who?" was all Austyn could say.

"She's over there, standing next to Sarah. I believe her name is Olivia," George replied, pointing to where Emily, Sarah, and Olivia were huddled.

"Okay. Cool, I guess, but what do you want me to do?" Austyn asked, still trying to sort through his confusion.

George couldn't believe his best friend was so dense. "Well, go over there and talk to her!"

13

Austyn stood in thought for a moment. He wanted to keep talking to D; he was rarely alone with her, and this was the perfect opportunity. He was about to tell George no but saw the gleam of happiness in his buddy's eyes and couldn't turn him down. "Okay," he finally said.

George was elated and grabbed Austyn's hand, forcing him to do the special handshake they had invented when they were little. He then looked to Emily and gave her a thumbs-up. He put his arm around Austyn's shoulder, and they walked towards Emily, Sarah, and Olivia. Austyn looked over his shoulder to D and saw that a guy had started a conversation with her. "Yep, just my luck," Austyn said to himself.

Once they reached the three girls, Austyn introduced himself to Olivia and engaged in small talk, which allowed George to focus on Emily once more. During their conversation, George learned that he and Emily had similar tastes in a lot of things, including music, movies, and food. They were having a great time and started planning a date to hang out. There was a definite chemistry between the two. Emily's body language put George's nerves at ease, and he was able to be himself with her.

D found herself in a pleasant conversation with a college student named Thomas. He was very smooth, complimenting her smile and telling her that her gray blouse made her beautiful brown eyes stand out. He was tall and outgoing, which was a trait that D liked. Thomas offered her a drink from the community ice chest that was set up and loaded with beer, wine coolers, and sodas.

When Thomas offered to grab her a drink, D said, "I'll have a Dr. Pepper, please."

"Sure thing, Damaris," Thomas replied with a smile.

D liked that Thomas said her full name. It showed her that he was trying which indicated his interest. Her name was uncommon, being that it was Biblical in origin and that her mother had chosen the Spanish pronunciation, *dah-maah-reese*. And while it had taken Thomas a few tries to say it correctly, once he had it, he insisted on using it.

During all of the conversations and good times, the hour grew nearer to eleven. Austyn had been periodically checking his phone for the time and also keeping tabs on D and her new friend. Olivia was nice and she was pretty too, but Austyn wasn't interested in her.

"I'll be back," Austyn said to Olivia.

"Okay, where ya' headed?" Olivia replied.

"Nature calls," Austyn shrugged, then added, "and I think I'm going to grab another beer." He then turned and walked by the ice chest to grab a beer, and passed where D and Thomas were talking hoping to grab D's attention. Going unnoticed and feeling a bit dejected, he continued on, walking into the woods to find a tree to "water."

Just then, a loud *bang* was heard nearby. The music stopped and everyone looked around. While panic hadn't spread just yet, a sense of curiosity and confusion was working its way through the crowd, dampening the jovial feeling of the night.

Bang! Bang! The definite sound of gunshots rang through the air followed by a deep, rumbling growl. The crowd broke up in an instant. Everyone was disappearing up the trail towards the vehicles. Sarah had already grabbed Emily, Olivia, and her other friends to start running back to the vehicle.

George ran to D who quickly said goodbye to Thomas.

"Let's go! Let's go!" George began to pull on D's arm.

"Where's Austyn?!" D shouted anxiously.

"I don't know, he was with Olivia!" George responded.

Bang! A fourth shot rang in the air followed by a deeper and much closer growl.

George and D were waiting at the trail entrance looking back towards the tree line in search for Austyn.

"RUN!" Austyn shouted as he emerged from the tree line in a rush, trying to simultaneously zip up his pants.

"Get to the truck, I'm right behind you!" Austyn yelled.

George and D ran up the trail and out of the trail head. They jumped into the truck and George turned the key and reversed from his parking spot, then stopped to wait for Austyn.

"Where is he?!" George shouted nervously.

"He's coming, he's coming!" D responded.

Bang! One last shot, much closer this time, echoed through the area.

"There he is!" D shouted, and she pointed to Austyn who was staggering towards the truck. He opened the rear passenger door and jumped in. "Go! Drive, George! Go!" Austyn shouted at George. George pressed the pedal to the floorboard of the truck; it fishtailed before stabilizing allowing him to get out of the parking area. The Chevy truck's motor hit 6000 RPMs and was roaring once again as the trio headed back towards the South IH-35 Highway.

Behind them, standing in the cloud of dust that remained from the freshly dug up dirt road, was a shadowy figure intently watching the quickly vanishing truck.

CHAPTER TWO: NIGHT TERRORS

"Austyn are you okay?" D asked with a worried look on her face.

"Yes, I'm fine," Austyn responded as he reached for his lower right leg.

His pant leg was torn, and he was bleeding.

"What happened to you?" D continued.

"I was taking a whiz by the creek when the first gunshot went off. I looked around into the trees from the direction of the sound, and when the second and third gunshot were fired, I saw the flash from the barrel of the gun. It was pointed in our direction. I was also able to make out a silhouette of a huge dog running ahead of the shooter. I thought it was a psycho with his big-ass dog coming to chase us off the property or something," Austyn told her while trying to catch his breath and calm himself down from the whole ordeal. "When I told you to run, I tripped over a stupid beer bottle. I could hear the damn dog getting closer and then another gunshot, so I tried to get up as fast as I could without looking back, but I wasn't fast enough. The dog got me and man did it hurt. It felt like It was trying to rip my leg off!"

D and George were listening intently to what had happened to their friend. When he didn't say anything more, they both asked, "And then what?!"

"I started trying to kick the thing off me. It was dark, so I didn't get a good look at it, but I knew it was big and mean. I could tell from its jaws clamped onto my leg. Then the last gunshot blasted like it was right behind me, and Cujo let me go. He must have been startled by his master's gunfire, but I decided not to stick around and find out. He let me go so I got the hell outta there!"

There was silence in the truck as the other two digested Austyn's story.

"Damnit!" Austyn shouted angrily.

"What happened, bro!?" George asked his friend with concern.

"I just bought these dang pants!" Austyn complained.

All three started to laugh. They were relieved that they got out of there when they did and that they were relatively unscathed. It was a strange night that ended with a close call.

Austyn laid down across the rear seat of the truck and put his hands behind his head and breathed a sigh of relief.

"Bro, I don't want my mom to freak out if she sees the tear on my pants and the blood on my leg, so I'm going to tell her that I'll be crashing at your pad tonight," Austyn informed George.

"Absolutely, bro. No problem. I get the bed though; you get the floor."

"After what I just went through and I got you extra points for talking to that Olivia girl, you better believe I'm sleeping on the bed!" Austyn retorted with a laugh.

"True dat! You earned bed privileges, but stay on your side, I'm not into any of that freaky stuff!" George joked.

"Okay, not weird at all," D added her thoughts on George's and Austyn's sleepover plans.

"Just make sure to put the toilet seat down, or you're going to wish that the dog didn't let you go!" D threatened.

Austyn acknowledged with a salute.

"So anyways, did you like that Olivia girl?" D asked Austyn.

"She was okay, definitely not my type though," Austyn answered.

"You really didn't like her, Austyn?" a puzzled George asked.

"Nah, she's not my type," Austyn repeated.

"Man, I was going to try and set us up on a double date at the drive-in next Friday," George said, relaying his scheme to Austyn.

"Dude, I don't want to lead the girl on," Austyn said. "Maybe D can come with us instead?"

Austyn looked to D, who turned to face him from where she sat in the front passenger seat.

"Excuse me? I have better things to do than spend another Friday with you two and almost get killed," she remarked.

"Oh, my bad. You probably have plans with frat boy." Austyn raised his eyebrows as he waited for her response.

"Frat b…oh! You mean Thomas?"

"I guess, if that's his name. I thought he would be called something like Biff, Kipp, or Ken, but I guess Thomas will do."

"Well, for your information —not that it's any of your business anyway —we did exchange numbers but we haven't made any firm plans. He's too far away anyways. I don't want to be driving up to Austin to go on dates," D replied.

"Thomas did kind of look like a jerk," George said, adding his two cents.

"You are both idiots!" D snapped, turning back around to face the front of the truck. George and Austyn laughed, and they all continued making fun of each other. After stopping for gas and grabbing a bite to eat, Austyn was able to buy rubbing alcohol and a bandage to dress his wound.

Just before 1 AM, the trio made it home to the Bala residence.

"Home at last. I'm so tired," D exhaustedly exclaimed.

"I'm not tired at all. I'm gonna see if Emily is awake," George said. He raised his arm to the sun visor above the driver side and clicked the garage door opener. The three adventurers made their way into the mudroom that was on the other side of the garage door. Once they got inside, they were met with a less than pleasant welcome.

"It's 1 AM! We've been up waiting for you!" a woman in her early forties berated. She was about to continue until she noticed that Austyn was there too.

"You should have called; you know how I worry," George and D's mother added a little more calmly.

"I told him we were gonna be too late getting home, mom," D replied, throwing her brother under the proverbial bus.

"Sorry mom, we just lost track of time," George began, but another voice entered the conversation, cutting him off.

"Did you fill up the gas?" an older, shorter, and heavier version of George asked.

"Yes, dad, all full," George answered.

"Hi daddy!" D said, hugging her father.

"Hi mija," he greeted.

"Well, glad y'all made it home safe, now we can go to bed," their father said. "Come on, my love, let's go to bed; the kids and my truck are safe."

"Okay," their mother said. "You can tell us about your night tomorrow," she added with a modicum of concern. Before heading to bed, she gave a goodnight hug to her children. "Goodnight, my loves," she added with a wave before retiring to the master bedroom.

"Goodnight, mom," George and D said.

"Goodnight, Mrs. Bala," Austyn said, keeping himself planted behind the kitchen island so his torn, blood-stained pant leg wouldn't be seen.

* * *

Once in their bedroom with the door closed, Letty frowned at her husband. She knew that they were adults by social standards, but George and Damaris were always going to be her babies. Not only that, but something about tonight wasn't sitting right with her. They were never home this late, without calling.

"I don't like that they got home so late, George," Letty complained to her husband as the two turned down the bed.

"Sweetie, they are home. They are safe. What more can we ask for? They are old enough to make decisions on their own," George Sr. stated in hopes of calming his wife. George Sr. was always the optimist; he knew that he and Letty had done the best job they could preparing Damaris and George for life outside of their home. He believed all you could do as a parent was make sure that your children knew to be respectful to others, that they worked hard for whatever they wanted in life, that they knew how to take a joke, knew when to say no, and, most importantly, that they knew they were loved.

"I know. I just wish you would have questioned them a little," said Letty as she climbed under the covers.

"We can ask them about everything tomorrow. It will give me a chance to make sure your son filled my truck up with gas," George Sr. added with a wink before plopping his head onto his fluffy pillow.

"Okay, fine. I know something happened, and I'm going to find out what," Letty said adamantly. The couple exchanged a goodnight kiss and closed their eyes.

* * *

D's and George's bedrooms were both located upstairs. They were in George's room talking about the craziness of the night while Austyn was taking a shower.

"Do you think something will come out on the news about that psycho?" D asked George.

"I'm not sure. It wasn't like we were in the middle of town. Unless someone called the cops, I don't think anything will be reported," George replied.

"You know mom is going to ask us questions about the night. She is going to want to know why we got home so late." D was concerned about worrying her mother; if she found out that they went to a party and a gun-toting psycho showed up, she'd never want to allow them to go anywhere again.

"Yeah, I know. Don't worry, though. We'll tell her the truth, well, mostly. We'll just leave out the part about the shooting and Austyn getting hurt. Besides, once she finds out that I met a girl *and* that the girl is from San Antonio, she won't be able to focus on anything except learning more about Emily," George responded.

"Very true," D said with a smirk. D knew George was right; their mom would want to know everything about Emily.

"I'll even tell her about Thomas," George stated with a grin. D stared at her brother and opened her mouth to response, but before she could, Austyn entered the room.

"What about frat boy?" Austyn commented.

"I already told you, his name is Thomas. He is going for his master's at St. Edwards in Austin," D retorted.

21

"Austyn, forget about Ken for a minute," George interrupted. He was finding it odd how bothered Austyn seemed to be by Thomas. He told Austyn that they were not going to tell his parents about the shooting or the crazy dog. Austyn agreed not to say anything about the creek, and, after some cajoling and finding out that D had hospital service hours to complete for her med school application and wouldn't be able to make it, he even agreed to the double date with Emily and Olivia that he had originally turned down.

After D left her brother's room, George checked Austyn's wound to see how bad it looked.

"Bro, you cleaned this up pretty good. It doesn't look that bad at all. But man, that dog had a big mouth," George commented.

Austyn was sitting in George's gaming chair and had his right leg elevated on a beanbag chair that looked like a baseball. The wound was about the size of a grapefruit. It looked deep and the skin around the teeth marks were purple and red.

"Does it hurt much?" George asked while poking at the meat in the center of the wound with a pencil eraser.

"Honestly, not really. If I wasn't looking right at it, I don't think I would know it was there," Austyn replied.

"Maybe you should get it checked out by a doctor. What if that freaking dog had rabies or something?" George's apprehension grew the more he thought about it.

"Yeah, maybe. I feel fine though. But you're probably right; the smart thing to do would be to get it checked out," Austyn said, agreeing with George. "I thought you were going to check on Emily?" Austyn asked.

"I did. We were messaging while you were in the shower. She said they all made it home okay," George replied.

"Cool, good to hear," said Austyn.

"We are going to talk more tomorrow; I caught her just as she was going to bed," George added.

"That sounds great," Austyn said, stretching his arms over his head.

"I want my clothes back too, bro. You can keep the underwear though," George joked. George climbed into bed on the right side of the mattress and

Austyn, after wrapping his wound with a bandage, climbed into the left side. They laid down head to feet to avoid any chances of unwanted bodily contact.

After they had fallen asleep, Austyn was tossing, turning, and sweating profusely in bed. He opened his eyes and suddenly found himself running through one of the hallways of the Slaughter Creek House of Terror. He couldn't see anything in front of him.

"Hello?!" Austyn yelled. "Hey, someone turn the lights on and let me out. I can't see crap!" he shouted into the darkness surrounding him. The sound of a door being forced open came from the end of the hallway.

"Hello? You need to let me out of here, dude! This isn't right, and it isn't funny!" Austyn pleaded with the unseen figure. He could hear the wood of the floor creaking telling him that whoever was in here with him was getting closer. Austyn dug into his pants pocket to get his cell phone and he noticed that he was wearing his torn, bloody pants again. Instead of finding his phone, his hand gripped a plastic rod-shaped object in his left front pocket. It was his green glowstick, still glowing faintly.

"What the..." Austyn mumbled as he stared at the glowstick. He was backed up against a wall and he could still hear the creaking of the floor. The hallway was beginning to fill with fog. Austyn extended the glowstick in front of him. After a moment of deafening silence, a wolf-like beast exploded through the fog and began to maul him.

"AHHHH...GET OFF OF ME!" Austyn yelled, falling from the bed with his arms flailing. He woke up to see George fast asleep in bed. From where he now sat on the floor, Austyn could see through the bedroom doorway and into the hallway. Two yellow, glowing objects glowing in the hallway caught Austyn's attention. He narrowed his eyes to get a better look through the dark and without warning in less than a second the same wolf-like creature pounced from the darkness of the hallway and landed on the bed. It ignored Austyn and began tearing up and mauling George this time, ripping out his throat and then turning to stare at Austyn with meat and blood falling from its mouth and dripping from its jaws.

"NO!!!" Austyn jumped out of bed yelling. George woke up and turned on the room light.

"Austyn, what's up?!" a startled George asked a frightened Austyn, unsure of what had just happened.

Austyn was distraught and confused. It had seemed so real. He looked at George's concerned face and then he saw the digital alarm clock on the nightstand; it read 3:33AM.

"Bro?" George called out to his friend, giving him a look that silently asked what happened.

"Sorry...I think I had a nightmare," Austyn said.

"A nightmare?" George repeated. He was concerned because, although he knew that night terrors were a real condition, in all their years of friendship he had never seen Austyn react like that to anything. Then he considered that it wasn't every day Austyn had been faced with gunshots from a mystery shooter and bites from a vicious dog. He nodded before saying, "You went through a lot tonight, bro. It is still fresh in your mind."

"You think so?" Austyn rubbed both of his hands down his face. He was still sweating, but his heartrate was returning to normal.

"For sure. Probably some kind of PTSD. Or if that dog that bit you had a disease, maybe it is some kind of side effect." George tried to make sense of the episode for his friend.

"Yeah, you're probably right," Austyn agreed after a moment's thought.

An angry and sleepy D exploded into George's room. "Idiots! Are y'all crazy?! Mom and dad are sleeping!"

"I'm sorry Damaris," Austyn apologized to D.

"He had a nightmare! He didn't do it on purpose, stupid!" George said in Austyn's defense. D took a step towards George and then thought better of it. She was too tired to deal with this; she hated having to wake up earlier than she absolutely had to. But she did feel bad that Austyn was hurt, so she just shook her head and turned around to leave George's room.

"Just shut up and go to bed!" D turned and quietly yelled at them. With all the commotion, the Bala's orange and white cat Autumn, wandered into the room. She leapt onto the nightstand and focused in on Austyn.

"Hey Autumn," Austyn called out kindly and took a step towards the cat. Autumn curled her spine and hissed aggressively at Austyn.

"Autumn! Cut it out! Get the hell out of here!" George yelled at his cat and ran her out of his room. George closed the room door and looked at Austyn who was still trying to figure out what was going on. "Bro, my cat hates you."

Austyn looked up at George and laughed. He was feeling better already, and he was relieved that it had only been a dream. He picked the pillow he was using up off the floor and placed it back on the bed and said, "I need some sleep."

George agreed. He turned off the room light and climbed back onto his side of the bed. "Don't even think about holding onto me if you get scared in the middle of the night," George said, trying to keep the slight chuckle from his voice.

"You know you want me," Austyn sarcastically responded, and he laid his head down onto the pillow and closed his eyes.

CHAPTER THREE: THE WOUND

Bright rays of sunlight were trickling in through the blinds of the bedroom window. Although his eyes were closed, Austyn could see the room brightening with the daylight. After having been woken by his nightmare, he had been able to sleep without incident for the remainder of the night. He turned onto his side and nestled in under the blankets a little further. Slowly, the aroma of freshly frying bacon and breakfast sausage made it into his nose, and he could hear the grease sizzling and the scraping of cooking utensils against pans.

"Austyn, what the heck is wrong with you, boy?" asked a perturbed George Sr.

Austyn opened his eyes to find himself standing in the middle of the kitchen wearing only the pair of boxer briefs George had given him. George's dad was sitting at the kitchen table and his mom was in front of the stove. They were both staring at Austyn, puzzled by his actions.

"Oh my God! I am so sorry Mr. and Mrs. Bala!" Austyn apologized before running back upstairs in a blaze and into George's room.

"Damn, that boy is weird," George Sr. commented with a chuckle. Letty nodded in agreement and returned her attention to the stovetop.

Back upstairs, Austyn pillaged through George's closet to find a pair of sweats. George walked into the room and saw his friend going through his closet.

"Morning, bro," he greeted Austyn.

"Dude, why didn't you stop me?" Austyn asked quietly.

26

"Stop you from what?" George asked, confused by Austyn's question.

"Are you freaking serious?!" D barged into George's room.

"What now?" George asked.

"Austyn, why the hell were you in the kitchen in your underwear?" D asked angrily.

"WHAT?! Mom and dad are in the kitchen!" George answered, shock coloring his features.

"Yeah, who do you think told me. They probably think that we got drunk or something last night," D said, glaring at Austyn.

"Austyn, really?" George turned his attention to his friend who was now dressed in some of George's clothes.

"I don't know what happened. I could smell the food, I'm starving, and next thing you know I'm standing damn near naked in front of your parents," Austyn told him.

George and D looked at each other and they couldn't help but laugh at what had transpired. They knew their parents wouldn't make too much of it, and, if anything, their dad would make fun of Austyn, not yell at him.

"I'll talk to mom and dad. I'll tell them that Austyn was sleepwalking and that he does it every now and then," George said with a shrug. He left the room and headed towards the kitchen. As he ran downstairs, he shouted, "Close your eyes, I'm naked!"

"Austyn seriously, are you okay?" D asked Austyn, concern in her eyes. She felt his forehead to check for fever. "You don't have a fever, so that's good. Are you going to get the bite checked out?"

"Yes, I'm going to go to one of those urgent care clinics after breakfast," he responded. He appreciated that D cared, and he loved the soft caress of her hand when she checked him for fever.

"Okay, make sure you go." D said, satisfied with his answer.

"Breakfast is ready!" Letty announced loudly.

"Let's go!" D said, motioning Austyn to follow her downstairs.

"I'm right behind you," Austyn told her. But before he followed, he went to the restroom to clean up properly. He had left his glasses on the sink counter the night before. He grabbed them and put them in the hoody pouch while he washed his face and brushed his teeth with the spare brush D had put out for him. When he was done, he rushed downstairs.

Austyn was welcomed with a proper good morning this time from the Balas. When everyone was finally present, they ate a wonderfully cooked breakfast while George did most of the talking, telling his parents about their haunted house adventure, his chance meeting with Emily, and the little get together at the creek. The family and Austyn laughed, enjoying their breakfast with one another, and Letty was very interested in learning more about Emily and Thomas. Austyn listened to George tell his story of their night out while thoroughly enjoying his food. There were a variety of flavors and he could decipher each and every one of them. Despite how delicious everything was and how much of it he ate, his appetite could not be quenched.

"This is delicious, Mrs. Bala!" Austyn complimented the chef.

"I can see that, Austyn. I'm glad you like it; do you want me to make you more food?" Letty asked genuinely.

"No, thank you," Austyn answered. He really wanted to say yes, but he did not want to overstep his boundaries.

"I didn't know you wore contacts, Austyn," George Sr. commented from across the table.

"I don't, sir," Austyn replied. He stopped eating and realized that he could see everything clearly, but he was not wearing his glasses.

"You're right, dad," George added. He was surprised that he hadn't noticed first, and even more surprised that Austyn himself hadn't noticed he did not have his glasses on since his vision rivaled that of a blind bat. *Oh well*, he thought to himself. This wouldn't be the strangest thing that has happened over the last twenty-four hours.

"I want to know more about this Emily girl," Letty cut in, changing the topic.

"I already told you, mom," George replied with a grin.

"How old is she? What school does she go to? What are her plans for college?" Letty continued firing off questions.

"I'm going to my room," D said with a laugh, and she excused herself from the table.

"Damaris, I want to know more about Ken too!" Letty shouted as D exited the kitchen.

"His name is Thomas, mother," D replied, jogging up the stairs and to her room.

"I have to be on my way as well," Austyn said, wiping his mouth. He put his dirty dishes in the sink and thanked the Balas for having him over and for breakfast.

"Bro!" George shouted at Austyn, hoping he would get the message and help him out of the spot he was in.

"I'll call you later, bro. Thanks for the clothes!" Austyn ran out the house laughing at his friend.

"Ass!" George shouted out the window at his running friend. He turned around and his mother was still sitting at the table patiently waiting to hear his answers.

Austyn only lived a few houses down from George so he slowed his jog to a walk. He reached into the pocket of the hoody he was wearing and retrieved his glasses. He put them on and his vision instantly blurred. He removed them again, and once more he could see with pristine acuity. Better than he ever could with his glasses on.

I could get used to this, Austyn thought to himself. He stowed his glasses away in the pocket and continued his walk home. When he arrived at his house, he gave his mother a good morning kiss and sat down for a second serving of breakfast.

"Good Morning mom!" Austyn said happily to his mother.

"Morning son, you look hungry." Austyn's mother Alicia said with a smile.

Austyn ate breakfast with his mother and told her about their experiences from the night before, excluding the close call at the end of the night.

When Austyn finally finished eating, he helped his mom clean the table and wash the dishes before running upstairs to grab his car keys and head to the urgent care. He told his mom that he was going to look for a Halloween costume and buy more candy for the trick-or-treaters.

Austyn hopped into his 2001 red Pontiac Firebird and drove out of the neighborhood. As he drove, the events from the previous night played over and over in his mind. He did not only think about the things that had happened when he was awake, but his mind drifted to the nightmare he had had. The creature that had stalked him in his dreams seemed so real. Suddenly, his cell phone rang and broke him out of his daze.

"Hello?" Austyn answered the call.

"Thanks for running out so fast and feeding me to the wolves you jerk," George berated his friend.

"Sorry bro, I had to go," Austyn began to explain.

"Yeah, yeah, whatever. Where you at?" George replied.

"I'm just pulling into the *Cure-All Urgent Care* center," Austyn informed him.

"Alright, call me when you're out. We need to set up the double-date," George said.

"Later," Austyn said then hung up the phone and, after parking, turned off his car. Austyn entered the building and signed in to be seen. Austyn began perusing through a magazine to pass the time while the waiting room TV droned on in the background. The article he had flipped to in the magazine was about the cycles of the moon, and how many cultures believe that the moon's influence can cause changes in behavior in people and animals.

"Late-breaking news from Austin, Texas," he heard from the TV. Austyn put the magazine down in his lap and turned his attention to the screen. "I'm Jesse Carrera and we're turning now to our field reporter Lupita Rivera from our affiliate in Austin." Austyn leaned forward, attention rapt, when he heard that it was news from Austin.

"Thank you, Jesse," the field reporter said. "I'm Lupita Rivera and we are coming to you live from Slaughter Creek, just south of Austin, Texas. A grisly discovery was made today when a fisherman came across the body of a nude male that had been shot multiple times, right here near the creek. There were several empty beer cans and bottles scattered on the ground which indicates that a gathering of some kind took place here last night. Neighbors near the creek said that they recalled hearing gunshots around 11 PM last night," Lupita reported.

Austyn couldn't believe what he was hearing. Someone had actually been shot by the maniac with a gun. He started to text George, but the door to the triage rooms opened, a nurse appeared and called out "Austyn Silver?"

Austyn put his phone away and followed the nurse. As he followed her silently, he could not shake the surreal feeling that the dead body that was found could have been him. When they reached the room, the nurse introduced herself as Lilly and took Austyn's vitals—which all appeared normal— and then she inquired about his reason for visiting today. When he told her about the wound and pulled up his pant leg, she began to remove the bandage and could see dried blood stains as she got closer to the skin, but when the bandage was fully removed, she stopped and asked, "What exactly happened to you?"

"I was bitten by a big dog last night," Austyn told her. He was laying down on the observation bed by this time. "Does it look bad?"

"Mr. Silver, there is nothing here," an agitated Lilly replied.

"What do you mean? There are teeth marks right—" Austyn stopped mid-sentence when he sat up and saw that the gruesome wound had completely disappeared in only a few hours. There wasn't even a scar. "It was there, I was bitten right there!" he insisted, pointing to where the bite marks had been that morning.

"There is nothing here, Mr. Silver, but know that we *will* be billing you for this visit. Especially since you've taken time and resources away from others in the waiting room who *do* need help." She sighed in annoyance. "Don't you kids have anything better to do than to play tricks on Halloween?" Lilly asked. She opened the door to the room and stared expectantly at Austyn.

Austyn pulled the leg of his sweatpants down and hopped down from the bed. "This isn't a joke," he commented to Lilly as he left the room and exited the building.

CHAPTER FOUR: HALLOWEEN NIGHT

The red Firebird engine slowed to a calm hum and parked against the curb of the Bala residence. He couldn't get ahold of George while he was driving, so he decided to show up at his house. The Bala family had known Austyn since he was six years old and they considered him another son. Years ago, George's parents had given Austyn a spare key to the rear patio door and told him he was welcome to come and go as he pleased. Key in hand, Austyn ran around to the back of the house to enter through the patio door.

The hurried young man quickly opened the backyard gate and ran inside where he was stopped by the sound of a bark. Alaska, the Bala's husky, was staring intently at Austyn from the rear corner of the yard. She was barking and growling like she had never done before. As a matter of fact, Alaska rarely barked. Only on certain occasions, when she was in a doggy spat with neighboring dogs, would she let out a couple of feeble barks. These barks were different, though. Alaska was being extremely defensive. She had never acted that way toward him and Austyn didn't know what to do. He tried to approach her, but she became more agitated, and even tried to jump over the six-foot privacy fence.

"Alaska, you too?" Austyn was beside himself. His confusion had turned to anger. "Shut up already!" he yelled at the auburn-colored husky. Alaska immediately stopped barking at his command and submissively laid on the ground.

Austyn frowned at her before inserting his key in the lock and letting himself into the Balas' home. Once inside, he ran upstairs to George's room and saw George laying on his bed talking on the phone.

"Bro, I've been freaking calling you for the last twenty minutes!" he yelled at his unaware friend.

George jumped out of bed holding his phone against his right ear and said "I'm gonna let you go, but I'll call you later." He ended the call with a "bye," and hung up.

"What is your problem?!" George asked angrily.

"My problem? My problem?! You're ignoring my calls for a chick you don't even know. Don't you think if I keep calling and texting you, I'm trying to get your attention for something important?!" Austyn answered heatedly.

"Dude, I was talking to Emily! My bad, what is so important?" George apologized and sat down on his bean bag.

"Look at this!" Austyn said excitedly as he raised his right pant leg and exposed an injury-free calf.

"What happened to the bite?" George asked, befuddled. He moved closer to inspect Austyn's calf. He had just seen the wound the night before, and now he couldn't even tell that anything had happened to Austyn.

"I don't know! The nurse removed the bandage, and then jumped all over my ass because she thought I was pulling a prank to waste her time," Austyn explained.

"Maybe it wasn't as bad as we thought?" George thought out loud.

"Georgie boy, it was bad. When it happened, I was in pain; believe me it was bad," Austyn rebutted.

"I don't know what to tell you, Austy. It may have happened but there's nothing there now. This is good news, right? You don't have to worry about rabies or a scar," George said, trying to put an optimistic spin on things.

Austyn appreciated George's optimism and had no choice but to accept that maybe the bite wasn't as bad as he first thought. Then Austyn remembered the news segment that he had seen in the waiting room at the urgent care center.

"Bro, there's something else," Austyn said in a somber tone.

"What else?" George asked.

"When I was in the waiting room at the urgent care center, the news was talking about a dead body that was found at Slaughter Creek," Austyn told him.

"What?!" George couldn't believe his ears.

"Yes, they found a nude male that had been shot multiple times near the creek. He was in a spot with a lot of empty beer bottles and cans," Austyn continued.

"Do you think that crazy guy did it?" George asked Austyn anxiously.

"Yeah, I think so," Austyn answered.

"Wow. I have to tell D; she is going to freak out," George replied.

"We are lucky to be alive." Austyn added.

"Wait a minute…I don't remember seeing a naked dude at the creek," George said as he was trying to make sense of the whole situation.

"Yeah, something like that would be hard to forget," Austyn agreed.

"I'll ask Emily to check with her cousin Sarah to see if any more details were released in Austin," George said, pulling out his phone to text Emily.

George and Austyn continued talking about the incident and going over possible scenarios about what really happened. They considered that since the male was nude, maybe it was a guy that was engaged in some kind of extramarital tryst with a married woman and that the two got caught by the husband, which they thought would explain the gunshots and the dog. The husband was mad, chased the adulterer, and murdered him. It was feasible. While they continued to discuss the news story Austyn had heard, they played video games until most of the day had gone by.

Austyn had been hungry for a while already, and when he saw that it was past 7 PM, he decided to call his mom to see what the plans were for dinner.

"Okay, mom. Yes, I'll be home soon. Love you too," Austyn finished the phone call with his mom and put his phone away. "Alright, bro, I'm gonna head home," he told George and stood up.

"Okay, bro. I'll let you know if I find anything else out." George put his game controller down, stood up, and the two, as they always did when they were parting ways, did their special handshake-shoulder bump.

"Cool," Austyn replied and walked out of George's room. On his way downstairs he saw Autumn, the Balas' cat, who was hiding underneath one of the couches gazing at him intently. Even though it was dark, he could see without issue. He heard a rapid beating, that intensified with every step he took down the stairs. When he made it to the landing of the staircase, Autumn hissed and ran off.

Dumbass cat, Austyn thought to himself. He was about to go out the back door, when he heard the humming of a small engine shutting down. Moments later he could smell the familiar expensive fragrance that D always wore.

"Hey Austyn!" D greeted Austyn happily. She was in a good mood. Based on her attire and the bag in her hand, she had just finished working out.

"Hi Damaris." Austyn returned the greeting with a smile.

"You leaving already?" she asked.

"Yeah, my mom has food waiting for me at home!" Austyn said.

"How is your leg?" D asked curiously.

"It is really good. In fact, it's completely healed. Can't even tell anything happened to me," he answered, lifting his pant leg to expose where the bite wound had been.

"Oh my God! That is not possible!" D said. She was astonished that there was no indication that anything had happened to Austyn.

"Yeah, George thinks that the bite wasn't as bad as we thought it was, that it was more superficial than anything else," Austyn relayed what he and George had talked about earlier.

"Well, you said that you weren't really in pain when we got home. Maybe it was just the panic of everything that took place that made it seem worse than it actually was," D suggested. While completing service hours at the hospital, D had seen plenty of what looked to be horrific wounds at first. But as she would clean the wound and prepare it to be examined by the doctor it would end up being much less severe than it originally appeared.

"True, and I feel real good right now. Just hungry," Austyn responded and felt his stomach grumbling.

"Okay, go home and eat. Tell your mom I said hi," D said, giving Austyn a hug before jogging upstairs.

Austyn waited and watched D as she went up the stairs, hoping she would turn around to look at him one more time. Once D disappeared out of view, he exited the back door of the house and saw that Alaska had remained a good distance away from him. Austyn emerged from the side gate and made his way to his car. It was dark and cool outside and he could hear the crinkles and crumbles of the auburn-colored leaves that had fallen to the ground. The laughter of children and Halloween music was in the air. Austyn's eyes dilated completely, and he was able to absorb every ray of light that was in the area. As he drove the short trip home, he could see clear as day.

Austyn made it to his house and saw that his older brother's blue SUV parked in the driveway and that a group of trick or treaters were receiving candy from Austyn's mom at their front door. A child dressed in a wolfman costume jumped out in front of Austyn and roared, startling Austyn and causing him to take a few steps back. Unbidden, images of the large dog running after him in the dark at Slaughter Creek flashed before his eyes.

The kid in the costume laughed and said, "I got him, I got him! I scared that wimp!"

Austyn watched the child meet up with his group of friends and run down to the next house. He could not believe that he let a kid in costume scare him.

He walked up to his mom and gave her a kiss on her forehead. "Hi mom."

"Hi Austyn, Eric is here with his family," Alicia said.

"Yeah, I saw that. Are they inside?" Austyn asked peeking around his mother, into the front door.

"No, he and Nat are taking little Erik and Izzy around the neighborhood," she told. "I left your dinner in the microwave, hun. How come you are not wearing your glasses?"

"Thanks mom. Oh," Austyn laughed nervously, forgetting he wasn't wearing his glasses. "I'm using contacts. I love you!" Austyn gave his mother another kiss and disappeared into the house. She frowned at his back. She knew Austyn did not like wearing contacts.

As Austyn warmed up his plate of chicken, mashed potatoes, and corn, he hoped his mom wouldn't think much about him saying he was wearing his contacts. He wasn't sure how he would explain the miraculous correction of his eyesight overnight.

"What's up!" Austyn's brother Eric said from across the kitchen as Austyn was putting his dirty dishes in the sink.

Austyn turned around to see his brother dressed like Frankenstein. He was followed by his wife Nat, who was dressed as the Bride of Frankenstein, and his nephews Erik and Izzy. The boys were four years apart in age with Erik being ten and Izzy being six. They were dressed as the Flash and Reverse Flash.

"Hi guys, happy Halloween! Come here you two speedsters, I'm the fastest in the universe!" Austyn greeted his family and began chasing his nephews around the kitchen. He caught his hyper nephews and scooped them both up with his arms.

Austyn loved seeing his nephews; his brother and his family lived in Louisiana, so he enjoyed every moment he got to spend with them. They were in town since Halloween was on a Saturday and the kids were off from school on Monday. Austyn sat down at the table with his brother's family and caught up with what has been going on in life.

Eric was almost eight years older than Austyn, so they weren't as close as most siblings since they were always in different stages of life. Even so, their mother Alicia always tried to push them to be like best friends. They knew it would make her happy, so they tried. Their mom was a hard worker, and seven years earlier when their dad lost his battle with cancer, she did everything she could to keep the family afloat. They both adored their mother and would do almost anything to bring a smile to her face.

It was a good night; one of the most memorable Halloween nights that Austyn had had since he considered himself too old to go trick or treating when he was thirteen years old. He played with his nephews and ate some of their candy, he joked with his brother on who was their mother's favorite son, and his mother and Nat were able to give each other pedicures and talk.

By ten o'clock, Eric and Nat wanted to get the kids to bed, and Austyn was feeling sleepy himself. He said goodnight to his family and made his way upstairs to shower before climbing into bed. Once he was in his bed, he picked up his phone that was charging on his nightstand and saw he had missed some text messages. The first message was from George letting him know that he should be expecting to hear from Olivia because Emily had given her Austyn's phone number. Austyn rolled his eyes and recalled that he had agreed to go on a double date to the drive-in with George and Emily.

The second text was from Olivia saying hi and happy Halloween and letting him know that she looked forward to hearing from him. Austyn responded to George with a middle finger emoji, and to Olivia with a goodnight and a smiley face. That done, he put his phone down, closed his eyes, and let himself drift off to sleep.

Austyn opened his eyes and he found himself standing next to the red ice chest at Slaughter Creek. It was completely silent and there was no one else around. He looked up at the full moon and it was blood red. He walked around the area and saw footprints in the sand with blood drops paralleling the prints. They were not human; they were paw prints that were larger than human feet. The prints went from that of a creature walking on four legs, to an upright creature walking on two legs, and finally to human footprints. The trail he followed led to a grassy area and the body of nude white male with gunshot wounds. Austyn couldn't believe what he was seeing. He looked around frantically to see if there was anyone who could help, but still, his surroundings were void of people. He searched for his phone to call the police, but it was nowhere to be found. He dropped to his knees and checked the body for a pulse. Nothing. Suddenly, he heard a tree branch snap causing him to stand up and scan the area. When he saw nothing around him, Austyn looked back down to the ground where the body lay. Slowly, the man on the ground opened his eyes and Austyn noticed that they were glowing a deep yellow. The man then opened his mouth to expose razor-sharp teeth.

Austyn heard rustling in the trees and a dark figure emerged with a pistol raised and pointed at him. Austyn put his hands up and shouted, "No, don't shoot!" The figure increased its pace toward him but stopped abruptly and yelled, "No, run!" before opening fire in Austyn's direction.

Austyn was going to do as he was told, but before he could move he felt a vice-like grip on his right leg followed by excruciating pain. The naked man that was supposed to be dead had taken a bite out of Austyn's leg with his razor-sharp teeth. Austyn fell to ground in pain, reaching for his leg. Just then, the man with glowing yellow eyes and a bloody mouth climbed on top of him and stared Austyn in the eyes and whispered, "Vous êtes le prochain!"

Austyn woke up panting in a cold sweat. He wanted to scream, but he was hyperventilating to the point that it was difficult to speak. His chest was pounding and his pulse was racing. In an attempt to calm himself down, he took slow deep breaths and closed his eyes. The sound of his own heart pounding gave way to the sound of a rhythmic whooshing. He opened his eyes and realized the sound was coming from the ceiling fan. He stood up and looked at himself in the mirror. *Something's wrong,* he worriedly thought to himself.

CHAPTER FIVE: THE ATTIC

Austyn couldn't sleep all night after his nightmare. Every time he closed his eyes, he saw the unknown man's face and heard the words he had uttered, "Vous êtes le prochain!" He had no idea what it meant, but he was going to find out.

Austyn looked at the time on his cell phone: 7:47 AM. He put on running clothes and met up with George at the end of their neighborhood street and the two went for their regular early Sunday morning run. George was extremely athletic, but he usually held back on Sunday mornings so Austyn could keep up with him. Not this time though. This time, George was doing all he could to keep pace with Austyn who was flying down their usual running course. Austyn didn't even appear to be struggling, the whole run seeming effortless for him.

When George made it back to the starting point, Austyn was stretching and looking incredibly proud of himself. It was the first time Austyn had finished before George on their five-mile jog.

"Damn Austyn! You were flying! What was your time?" George asked while trying to catch his breath.

Austyn looked down at his smartwatch and he couldn't believe what he was seeing. He looked up to a hunched over George and said, "Bro, I just ran five miles at a clip of four minutes and eleven seconds per mile!"

"What? How can that be?" George straightened up. He was awestruck by Austyn's time. Austyn averaged about nine minutes per mile, and on his best run he ran three miles at eight minutes and forty-nine seconds per mile.

"I don't know, bro; maybe the GPS on my watch is messed up or something," Austyn stated, tapping the face of his watch.

"I don't know about that, but you spanked me today," George said, congratulating Austyn with their custom handshake. "I need a shower and some breakfast," George added and rubbed his stomach.

"Cool, I'll pick you up in an hour," Austyn said to George and the two separated and went to their homes to shower and get ready.

* * *

When George finished showering and getting ready, he went downstairs where he was met by his very cheerful mom.

"Good morning, mijo!" she lovingly said, giving him a hug and a kiss on the cheek.

"Good morning, Mom!" George said and embraced his mom.

"How was your run?" Letty asked.

"It was good, except for one thing," George replied.

"What happened?" she asked.

"Austyn beat me today," George started. "He didn't just beat me, he smoked me. He ran a four-minute mile for five miles!" George explained.

"Oh, well that isn't a bad thing. Austyn is in good shape and works out, just like you," Letty said and grinned at her son, trying to ease the jealousy she could sense.

"Yeah, I know. But I run with him every week. He isn't slow, but he is definitely slower than me. He ran at almost an Olympic pace...and he didn't even look winded and he barely broke a sweat. I think he was holding back." The more George thought about it, the more confused he became.

"Well, you should be happy for your friend. Maybe he has been the one holding back on all of your runs." Her reply was met with a bemused expression on George's face.

"Anyway, we are gonna go get something to eat," George said, not finding amusement in his mother's comments.

"Where are we going?" George Sr. asked as entered the kitchen.

"You're not going anywhere, old man. Austyn and I are going to get some breakfast," George responded, throwing a few shadowboxing punches at his dad.

"Okay, well when you get back, this old man has some young man chores for you to do," George Sr. said with a grin.

"Aw, Dad! I wanted to relax today," George complained.

"You've relaxed all weekend, fool! I need your help getting stuff out of the attic so your mother can hold a garage sale at your grandparent's house next weekend. It won't take long. Besides, the sooner you st—"

"Yeah, I know dad," George said, interrupting his father's words. "The sooner you start, the sooner you'll finish." George sighed mocking his dad. "Okay, you're right. After breakfast, I'll drag Austyn along to help as well." George couldn't help but smile at his father. Anytime George complained about something that was going to be time consuming or boring, he was met by his father's response of, "The sooner you start, the sooner you'll finish." It was simple, but true.

"That's my boy!" George Sr. slapped his son on the back. George saw through the family room window that Austyn had pulled up to the house.

"Austyn's here, love y'all!" George waved bye to his parents and went out the door. He jumped in the car and looked at Austyn with a sinister smile.

"What?" Austyn asked, knowing something was up.

"Nada, just hope you still have energy left after that run you had," George responded innocently.

"For what?" Austyn asked, narrowing his eyes at his friend.

"You'll find out soon," George responded and put his seat belt on. Austyn silently accepted George's response and he turned the volume to his car radio up.

The red Firebird with heavy metal music blasting from its speakers pulled in the parking lot of B Jones Restaurant. George and Austyn loved the breakfast from B Jones. The sausage steak platter was to die for. They signed in with the hostess and waited to be seated.

Austyn did everything in his power to concentrate on the conversation he and George were having about the attic clean up after breakfast, but the aromas from all the different dishes being served were overwhelming his sense of smell.

"Dude, you alright? Ever since that night at the creek you've been acting weird," George said, having noticed Austyn's behavior. He seemed on edge and his eyes followed every plate of food that passed him.

"Yeah man, I'm just hungry and I didn't get a lot of sleep last night," Austyn said, coming back to himself.

The hostess called for their party of two to be seated and they followed her to an empty booth. They placed their drink order while they waited for their waitress to arrive to take their food order.

"Sorry, bro. I didn't get a lot of sleep last night either. That Thomas dude came to the house last night to take D to dinner. There is something about that guy that I don't like, I don't know what it is," George said, sharing his thoughts on the guy that D was currently dating. "And I stayed up late talking to Emily, which was great. She said her cousin knows Thomas and he is supposed to be a decent guy. Then, I invited her out in a few weeks to the drive-in to watch that new horror film *Clowntown*."

"D went out with frat boy?" Austyn asked with a look of defeat. The waitress arrived at the table with their drinks and proceeded to take their food order.

"Yeah, they went to eat," George said, frowning a bit at Austyn's dejected look when hearing about D's date. "I didn't like it, but, like I said, Emily says he's a decent dude. I trust her opinion," George finished with a shrug before taking a drink of his water. "Anyway, did you talk to Olivia?" he asked, changing the subject to their possible double date.

"Uh...yeah. She texted me and I responded last night," Austyn replied.

"Well, call her today and get to know her so you can ask her out!" George said excitedly.

"Don't you want to be alone with Emily?" Austyn asked.

"Of course I do, but you are my bro. We had already made plans to watch *Clowntown*, I'm not going to break my plans with you. Besides, I want you to have a girl in your life too, that way there's always the possibility of double dates and we can still hang out. Blood brothers forever, Austyn."

"Alright, alright. I'll give her a call after we finish helping your dad with the chore you volunteered me for," Austyn laughed and threw his napkin across the table to George.

After the talk of double dates and girlfriends, Austyn told George about the nightmare that he had last night and how real it felt. He told him how every detail about the creek in the nightmare was accurate, except for the mysterious man with the gun and the nude male that bit his leg. Austyn repeated what the man said to him. He didn't know what language it was, but he could hear the words as clear as day. George was intrigued by the nightmare. It was clear to him that Austyn was definitely suffering from a bit of PTSD from what had happened to him at Slaughter Creek. Before George could say anything more about it, though, the food arrived and they both began to eat. Austyn changed the subject and asked George about Emily. He wanted to know more about the girl that had caught the interest of his best friend. The remainder of breakfast went by as usual, with Austyn spending the majority of the time teasing George. George paid for breakfast because Austyn finished the run first. Austyn had no complaints; he was happy not having to pay.

They left the restaurant, satisfied with their breakfast, and headed back to George's house. This was the first time that Austyn had felt like himself since the incident at the creek and he knew George had a lot to do with that. George knew what to do to make him laugh and to pull him out of the doldrums.

When they got to George's house, they sat down in the living room to watch some football with George's dad. As soon as their backsides hit the couch, George Sr. turned the TV off.

"Okay, half-time," George Sr. said. He stood up from his recliner and looked at the boys. "Let's do it!" He walked up the stairs and climbed into the attic, followed by George and Austyn.

"What are we supposed to do dad?" George asked as he brushed spider webs out of his face.

"Grab the boxes labelled junk, and anything that belonged to you or your sister that you are not going to want to keep. Take them down to the stairwell and we will load them in my truck when we are done," George Sr. explained.

George and Austyn looked around at all the boxes filling the attic; most of them said junk in thick black marker. George Sr. gave the boys a thumbs-up and began climbing out of the attic.

"Dad, where are you going?" George asked his exiting dad.

"Oh, I'm going to finish watching the game," George Sr. responded.

"But what about the —"

"You boys are young and strong," George Sr. said. "I'm an old man, I need to rest," he chuckled and left his son and Austyn in silence. They looked at each other in amazement; they had been scammed by George's dad.

Just as they were about to start rummaging through the boxes, George's dad added one more thing.

"Be careful with the spiders!" he yelled up the stairs.

George hated spiders and his dad knew it. Austyn couldn't help but laugh when George dropped the box that he had just picked up.

The boys worked hard, eventually turning the chore into a competition to see who could take out the most boxes. Everything was going well until Austyn dropped a box and let out a yell. "OW! SHIT!"

George stopped what he was doing and ran to Austyn who was holding his right hand. Austyn was bleeding and clearly in pain. George looked at the box that Austyn had dropped and a silver-plated letter opener that had belonged to his grandfather had punctured through the box.

"What did you do, dumbass?" George asked his friend with a laugh.

"It's not funny, that thing hurts. It's burning too!" Austyn replied in pain.

George got a closer look at Austyn's hand and saw that while the wound on Austyn's hand was small, it was very red and his entire hand was hot.

Letty had heard the yell from the kitchen and ran upstairs to check on the boys. "What happened, is everything okay?!" she yelled up at them, about to climb into the attic.

"We're okay mom. Austyn cut himself on grandpa's old letter opener," George explained to his mom.

"Oh no. Austyn come down here so I can take a look and clean it up for you," Letty called out.

"Okay, Mrs. Bala. I'm on my way," Austyn replied and climbed down the ladder.

George was alone in the attic. He looked around and realized he was going to have to finish the rest on his own. Sighing heavily, he kicked the box Austyn had dropped and it tore open spilling its contents to the floor.

"Just my luck!" George shouted at himself. He crouched down to start gathering all of the objects and realized everything was silver. It seems his grandpa had been quite the silver enthusiast. There were silver-plated pens, plates, silver cufflinks, and silver coins. He grabbed the coins and said, "Piggy bank, here I come." He collected the other items and placed them on top of a box, and put the silver-plated letter opener in his pocket. Meanwhile, downstairs in the kitchen, Austyn was being tended to by Mrs. Bala.

"Ouch! Sorry, Mrs. Bala, it just burns," Austyn groaned as Mrs. Bala was cleaning the cut.

"It's okay. I'm used to dealing with big babies with small injuries," she said with a smile.

"I heard that, sweetie," George Sr. shouted from the living room.

Mrs. Bala rolled her eyes and put a Band-Aid on the cut. "You're all ready to go, Austyn."

"Thank you!" Austyn replied. He felt his left hand as he took his leave from Mrs. Bala. The burning had subsided, but he still rubbed over the Band-Aid to sooth the wound. Even he was surprised that a small nick had caused him so much discomfort and pain. Just as he was nearing the stairs, George appeared and pronounced that all the junk was out of the attic.

"Great! Let's put it in the truck now," George Sr. said, getting up out of his recliner once more. Despite the dull pain in his hand, Austyn finished helping George and his father.

"Thanks for the help, Austyn! It seemed like you did more with one hand than me and Georgie combined," George Sr. joked.

"Speak for yourself, you were slowing me down, Dad," George replied.

"No problem, Mr. Bala," Austyn replied politely.

George Sr. closed the tailgate to the truck and climbed into the passenger side of the truck.

"Hey, Gramps, you got in the wrong side; the driver's side is the other door!"

George said, making fun of his dad.

"No, I'm on the right side. You're driving, fool!" George Sr. answered.

"What?! But me and Austyn were —" George didn't bother finishing his sentence when he saw the look on his dad's face in the passenger door mirror.

"I think you better go, bro," Austyn advised George.

"Yeah, I don't want to put the old timer in a bad mood," George agreed.

"You know I'm only forty-five years old!" George Sr. interjected.

"Call Olivia while I'm gone. Get to know her, invite her for *Clowntown*," George added while he climbed into the truck.

"I will, I will," Austyn said and waved to George and his dad as they drove away.

CHAPTER SIX: MOTHER'S INTUITION

Austyn was about to walk to get into his car when D pulled into the driveway. She had gone grocery shopping for her mother and had a few bags in her small plum-colored SUV.

"Let me help you with those," Austyn said and grabbed six bags of groceries.

"Thanks, Austyn. I just passed my dad and George. My little brother did not look happy," D remarked as she followed Austyn into the house to leave the groceries on the kitchen table. When they got inside, D spotted her mother. "Hi Mom! There are a couple more bags in the car, I'll bring them in!" D hugged her mom quickly before turning to go back outside.

"Wait up, I'll help!" Austyn said and jogged after D.

Letty stood in the kitchen and smiled. She had begun to suspect that Austyn liked D. He was always nice to her and was always offering to help her, even though she was mean to him sometimes. Letty thought Austyn was a good kid and knew he would treat D right, but she thought the age difference might eventually become problematic. Nonetheless, she knew that D could do a lot worse than finding someone like Austyn. She sighed and started to put the groceries away.

Outside, D was growing increasingly annoyed with her brother's friend.

"I got it, Austyn, it's only three bags," D said in a huff and shut the rear hatch of her vehicle.

"I know but let me grab them for you anyway." Austyn took the bags from D and the two locked eyes.

"You know, you have nice eyes. I guess I never noticed because you are always wearing your glasses," D complimented Austyn.

"Thank you. My sight has improved over the past few days for whatever reason, and I don't need my glasses anymore," Austyn responded happily.

"George told me about the dead guy they found at the creek. I couldn't believe it. Are you feeling okay still? You know…after everything?" D asked.

"Yes. I was shocked when I saw the news as well, but I feel good. Apart from the fact that I'm having trouble sleeping. Realistic nightmares wake me up and keep me up all night it seems," Austyn replied.

"More nightmares?" D asked interestedly. As part of her major area of study, D had taken psychology classes and had written her dissertation on the interpretation of dreams and nightmare. She opened the door for Austyn, who was still holding the last three few grocery bags, and they walked into the house.

"Yes, weird and realistic," Austyn answered.

As he placed the bags on the table, D noticed that Austyn was favoring his left hand and was wearing a bandage. She was about to ask him about it but thought better of it in that moment. Instead, Austyn and she began helping Letty put away all of the groceries.

"Thank you, mija! You saved me a trip to the store. Can you put everything away while I fold the laundry?" Letty asked, already on her way out of the kitchen. "Bye Austyn!"

"So, sit down, tell me about the nightmares," D said to Austyn, urging him to recall the nightmares. And so, Austyn told D about the nightmares, starting with the one he had the night before Halloween. D listened intently and asked Austyn for more specific details about the dreams. After hearing about his nightmares, she analyzed them based on the research for her dissertation.

"Austyn, I'm not a shrink, but I think what happened at the creek really scared you, and deeply, and now subconsciously you are running away from something, or you feel like something is chasing you to cause you harm," D suggested.

"Wow, well thank you Dr. Will, how much do I owe you?" Austyn jokingly responded, referencing Dr. Will, a popular TV psychiatrist on their local stations. He appreciated D listening to him and caring enough to try and help him.

"Shut up, stupid," D laughed and slapped Austyn's hand.

"Ow!" Austyn grunted holding his left hand.

"Austyn, I'm sorry! I was playing around," D apologized. She felt bad for hurting his hand.

"No, it's not your fault. Me and your brother were clearing out the attic earlier today and you know how we are," Austyn began to explain.

"Yes, you are idiots," D interrupted with a grin.

"Yes, we are. Well, we were trying to see who could get the most boxes down from the attic first —I won by the way — and then I picked up this one box, and when I tried to squeeze it for a better grip, this letter opener punched through the side of the box and stabbed my hand," Austyn finished his explanation.

"Oh, that stinks!" D added. "Can I take a look at it?" She pulled his hand toward her softly and removed the Band-Aid.

"Your mom cleaned it for me." Austyn winced as D scanned the cut.

"It's really not that big of a wound at all, but even paper cuts can cause a lot of pain. It looks fine; you should be okay. It is just a pain tolerance threshold now." D replaced the Band-Aid and let Austyn's hand go.

"Thanks. So, I heard you had dinner with that Thomas guy last night," Austyn said, awkwardly changing the subject.

"My brother is worse than a girl with the gossip. Yes, Thomas' parents live in Selma, so after he visited them, he asked me out to dinner," D answered.

"How was it? If you don't mind me asking." Austyn asked hoping for the worst.

"It was nice. He is mature and has goals, which is a breath of fresh air, and we went to a Mexican restaurant," D answered.

"Oh, Mexican food," Austyn said with a smile. He knew that despite being of Mexican-American descent D didn't really care for Mexican food unless it was homemade. "You hate Mexican food."

"I don't hate Mexican food, I just prefer to eat it homemade," D corrected with a laugh.

"I better get going," Austyn said and stood up from the table.

"Okay, I'll see you later," D replied and stood up to give Austyn a hug. He turned and was about to walk out the door when D said, "You're next."

Austyn stopped in the doorway and turned to look at D with a puzzled expression. "Huh?"

"Vous êtes le prochain. The words from your dream. It's French for you're next," D explained.

"Thank you." Austyn nodded his head and walked out the door, D watching him as he went.

She smiled to herself. Austyn was a good guy and a good friend. He didn't deserve to be so freaked out over his nightmares. She sighed to herself, hoping Austyn's nightmares would pass, as she walked to her parent's bedroom to give her mom a hand with the laundry.

Letty was smiling from ear to ear as she folded a pair of George Sr.'s shorts.

"What?" D asked curiously.

"Nothing, mija," Letty answered and continued to fold clothes.

"Okay, Mom, what? Tell me?" D knew that her mom had something she wanted to say.

"It's just that I see the way Austyn looks at you, and the way he treats you. He likes you, mija, a lot," Letty told her daughter.

"Oh Mother! You think every guy likes me!" D responded, annoyed by her mom's comments.

"Mija, he likes you," Letty stated matter-of-factly.

"Really?" D was mystified by the notion. She remained quiet as she continued to fold.

"How was dinner with Thomas last night?" Letty asked her daughter.

"Who…oh…I mean it was good," D responded distractedly.

D had never thought of Austyn as anything more than her brother's friend. She wasn't blind, though; she thought he was attractive, and she knew he was smart, but he was young. *My mom Is crazy*, she told herself. *There is no way that Austyn likes me.*

* * *

51

A few houses down the block Austyn returned home. He walked in and saw that Eric and family had their luggage in the living room.

"We're gonna get going, Austyn. We've got a long drive ahead of us," Eric said and gave Austyn a hug. "Take care of mom," Eric added as he picked up his suitcase.

"I will, Eric," Austyn answered. He turned and gave a hug and kiss to Nat. "Sorry you have to put up with being trapped in a car for eight hours with my brother."

"It'll be fine. I plan on sleeping most of the drive," Nat responded with a smile.

"Bye Uncle Austyn!" Erik and Izzy said simultaneously.

"I'm going to miss you!" Erik added and gave Austyn a big hug.

"Me too!" Izzy joined in on the hug.

"I love you guys. Take care of your dad, he's old and grouchy," Austyn said to the brothers.

"We will!" They laughed.

"Daddy's old!" Izzy shouted.

"Oh, thanks Austyn. Gonna be a fun ride home now," Eric responded sarcastically.

Austyn and his mother stood on the front porch and watched as his brother and family backed out of the driveway and made their way out of the neighborhood. Austyn's mom mentioned that they were planning to return for Christmas which Austyn was happy about. He missed his brother living close by.

Before Austyn could head back inside, Austyn's mom asked, " Were you at the Bala's this whole time?"

"Me and George went to eat breakfast after our run, and we helped his dad with clearing out the attic," Austyn replied.

"That's good, Austyn. I'm glad the Balas care for you like they do." She patted him on the shoulder and walked inside.

"Is everything okay mom?" Austyn asked, following his mother into the house. He sensed that something was wrong.

"Yes, Austyn. I've just had this feeling all weekend that something bad is coming." she frowned at him. "It's the same feeling I had before your father passed," she added.

"Really? How bad do you think this something is?" Austyn asked, wanting to know more.

"It's hard to explain. I just have a feeling that my child is in danger," she said, her eyes tearing up.

Austyn hugged his mother tightly. "We're fine mom. I'm right here and we just saw Eric. We are both fine. Don't cry, please," Austyn consoled his mother.

"I know, baby boy," she sniffed. "Maybe it's just the season. Your father always loved this time of the year," she said, trying to make sense of her feelings.

"Mom, everything is okay," Austyn said and kissed his mom on the forehead.

"What happened to your hand, Austyn?" She said suddenly, noticing the band-aid on his hand.

"I cut myself with a letter opener at the Bala's," he explained.

"It must have been some sharp letter opener," his mother joked.

"Yeah, George said it was his grandpa's silver-plated opener," Austyn replied.

"How is George doing?" she asked.

"He is good; he was a little annoyed because his dad made him help with some chores," Austyn answered with a laugh.

"And Damaris?" she added with a knowing smile.

"She is good mom," Austyn answered shortly.

"She has grown into a beautiful young lady, don't you think? She has a good, strong family foundation, and she's ambitious," Austyn's mother continued. "She is going to make some man very happy."

"Yeah, I believe she will too," Austyn added with a fake smile.

"Why do you do this to yourself?" she questioned Austyn.

"Do what?" he answered defensively.

"Hide your feelings. Your father was younger than me and he made his feelings known, and because of that single moment of courage we went on to live a beautiful life and have two wonderful sons."

"Mom, I don't know what you are talking about." Austyn shook his head in disagreement.

"I see the way you look at her. When she comes over with George, I see the way you act around her," she said.

"Mom, even if you were right —and I'm not saying that you are —Damaris met someone," Austyn replied.

"So? They're not married," she commented sneakily. "Heaven helps the man who fights his fears, my son," she added and gave her son a kiss on the cheek. She left Austyn sitting in the living room pondering his inner feelings about D and about the ominous feelings that were weighing heavily on his mom.

CHAPTER SEVEN: "ROID RAGE"

Austyn's heart was racing. He didn't know what to do. Sweat was beading on his brow and running down his cheek. He was trapped with nowhere to run, and to make things worse, George and about twenty other people were in the same predicament. It was a cold, life-draining atmosphere. Then a familiar and unwelcomed voice broke the tense silence in the air.

"Five more minutes, people!" Mr. Morales declared to his class full of freshman college students that were taking their last major test before finals. The class let out a desperate moan and the scratching of pencils intensified. It was the Wednesday before Thanksgiving and the calculus professor was sending his students off with a bang.

George put his pencil down and closed his test booklet. He was good at math, but this test was a doozy. Still, he was confident he'd receive a high grade. Austyn, on the other hand, was struggling to get through. What made the whole situation worse was the constant rubbing of erasers and etching of pencils around him.

"Time's up! Pencils down. Pass your tests and answer sheets forward!" Mr. Morales announced. A student raised her hand. "What is it Lhea?"

"Are you going to have the test grades posted today?" Lhea asked hopefully.

"Not today," he answered in usual dry tone and mocking laugh. He looked at the clock on the wall and raised both arms. "Class dismissed. See you on Monday; come ready to work."

George waited outside the classroom for Austyn who walked out scratching his head.

"I hate calculus, and Mr. Morales is a complete douche!" he lamented to his friend.

"Yeah, he's definitely a jackass," George agreed.

"I bombed it man, I know I did. Fifty percent of my final grade. He knew what he was doing, he could have given us this test on Monday," Austyn complained.

"I think I did okay on it," George said modestly, he didn't want to let Austyn know that even though the test was long, he hadn't found it too difficult. As they were walking to their vehicle in the parking lot, they saw Mr. Morales get into to his gray Nissan truck and drive off.

Austyn was perturbed by the test, but other than that, things had been great for him over the past few weeks. The nightmares seemed to have stopped and he felt like he was bursting with endless amounts of energy. He had even increased his bench press weight at the gym from 225lbs to 365lbs, but that was the maximum he could go; no one was able to spot him beyond that weight. He had gone for his yearly vision checkup and his vision acuity improved from 20/70 to 20/10, which the eye chart wasn't designed to test beyond. To top things off, because of his performance on their runs, he hadn't had to pay for Sunday breakfast for three weeks straight.

They climbed into his car and Austyn started the engine, grateful to be leaving college behind for the long holiday weekend.

"So, are you ready for Friday?" George asked Austyn.

"Yeah, the movie should be good," Austyn responded.

"Yes, but I mean you and Olivia," George grinned and raised his eyebrows.

"She is nice, it will be fun. Thankfully, her folks live in New Braunfels, close to the theatre," Austyn added plainly.

"My dad said it's about damn time that we are going to have chicks other than D in the truck," George laughed, repeating his dad's words.

Austyn laughed. "Your dad is cool! He busts your balls all the time," he replied.

"I know. Man, I love that old fart!" George said happily.

The Firebird continued down the road and Austyn's mind wandered, landing on the words, "You're next!" While the nightmares had ceased, he still thought about the French words that had been spoken in them. How had a coherent French sentence ended up in his dream? He didn't know French, and had never taken any French classes, so for his dream to have French words in them was strange. Though the last three weeks had been uneventful, curiosity about the nightmares visited him on a regular basis. As much as he'd wanted to talk to George about everything, he hadn't said much. George had been talking more and more with Emily, getting to know her, and Austyn didn't want to bother his friend with unnecessary worries.

George looked out the window of the Firebird. He was excited for the weekend. He loved Thanksgiving, but he was especially looking forward to Friday. He and Emily had gotten closer over the past few weeks, but they hadn't been able to see each other because of school schedules and family plans. They did talk to each other every day over the phone and sent flirty, emoji-filled text messages continuously throughout the day, but it wasn't the same as seeing her in person.

The boys pulled into Austyn's driveway and stepped out of the car. They had planned an evening of snacks and *Call to Action* gaming, their favorite first-person war simulation game. Austyn opened the front door to the house, and they walked in and were greeted by Austyn's mom.

"Hi boys! How was the calculus test?"

"Hello, Mrs. Silver. It was tough, but I think I did alright," George answered and turned to Austyn who was closing the door.

"Hi, Mom. Mr. Morales hates freshman," he huffed. "The test was difficult, but I think I passed."

"Well, what's done is done. Don't fret over it this weekend," she said with a smile, trying to lessen her son's worry.

"I know, Mom. It won't ruin the weekend," Austyn replied.

"George, when you get home, please tell your mom to let me know if she needs me to bring anything else besides the cheesecake and ham," said Alicia.

The Silvers spent Thanksgiving at the Balas' house whenever they didn't visit Eric in Louisiana. The two families were close and had become even more so after Austyn's father, Joseph, passed away.

"Will do, Mrs. Silver!" George replied with a smile. He and Austyn were already halfway up the staircase.

"Pizza is ordered and on the way, boys!" she shouted up the stairs as they disappeared into Austyn's room. She turned to the walk away, and she heard both boys shout "Thank you!"

It was a fun-filled night, full of extra cheesy pepperoni pizza and buffalo wings, and the duo dominated their *Call to Action* battles.

Thanksgiving morning arrived and the Bala house was abuzz with activity. Letty was on her yearly mission to satisfy her family's holiday feast along with D whom was learning from the best. D wanted to learn everything possible about cooking from her mom before she was out on her own.

The turkey had been brining for two days and was ready to go into the oven for its four-hour transformation into pure succulence and tenderness. The potatoes were boiling on the stove along with the homemade brown gravy. Everything was on track for the Balas' Thanksgiving meal to be served at their traditional time of 2 PM.

It was just about time to serve the feast when the doorbell rang. D excused herself from the table and went to answer the door. Austyn followed her with his eyes as she left the dining room. She rarely used makeup but, being as it was a holiday, she had put on a light touch that accentuated her features. She was wearing a turtleneck sweater in a smattering of fall colors, a brown skirt that went down to her knees, and brown boots.

She looks stunning today, Austyn thought to himself.

George Sr. walked into the dining room with the turkey all carved up and placed it in the center of the table surrounded by all the dressings. D followed her father into the dining room, and, to Austyn's dismay, she was accompanied by Thomas. D formally introduced Thomas to everyone and directed him to the vacant seat next to her own.

"Oh great," Austyn mumbled under his breath. He tried to ignore his feelings of disappointment, and the touch of rising jealousy, but it was difficult. It became even more difficult every time D laughed at Thomas' jokes or touched his arm. And George wasn't helping the situation by getting along with his sister's invited guest. Austyn's frustration festered as he ate, growing into anger. He began to have visions of flipping the table over and beating Thomas to a pulp. His hands curled into a fist under the table, and he couldn't stop his legs from bouncing up and down.

Thomas was talking about his ambitions for after he completes his Master's. He was majoring in criminal justice and planned to become a lawyer. He began to speak about how police brutality was a real issue and he wanted to specialize in those types of cases.

"It is basic human decency that those in charge of the public's safety do everything in their power not to hurt citizens but to help them. Instead, most of these bullies who are given specialized training to incapacitate a citizen, do more harm than good," Thomas said, explaining his stance on the subject.

"So, tell me, Thomas, are these officers who risk their lives every day and who are shown so little respect by the public at large in today's society —because of bureaucrats like you —supposed to just stand there and let suspects do whatever they want?" Austyn rebutted. While Thomas hadn't attacked him personally, Austyn took offense to Thomas' words, seeing as his father had been the deputy of Bexar County for seventeen years prior to his death. Before Thomas could get a word out, however, Austyn continued. "Officers are trained to use any means necessary to end a threat, but before it gets to that point, they have to follow the continuum of force. They don't go out looking to hurt people, but if someone is resisting lawful commands and becomes a threat to themselves, the people around them, or the officers, the officers have to engage and take that person into custody. If that happens, it's their own damn fault! But as long as these criminals claiming to be law-abiding citizens have lawyers like you to go to, officers will be hesitant to do the job that they were sworn to do. And you know what? I don't blame them!" Austyn looked at his mother and excused himself from the table. He apologized to the Balas and left the dining room.

"Austyn's dad was a deputy for Bexar County," D explained to Thomas.

"I had no Idea. I am sorry if I offended anyone here," Thomas said, apologizing for his statements.

"It's fine, dear; you had no way to know," Alicia replied to Thomas. She looked at Letty and said, "I'm going to go check on him. I'll be back to help with the cleanup."

59

"No, it's fine, Alicia, we'll take care of it." Letty stood up and gave Alicia a hug.

"I'm gonna go check on Austyn too," George said, and he stood up from the table.

"I think he would appreciate that, George," Alicia said, and the two left the house together and walked the short distance to the Silver residence.

"That was about as mad as I've seen Austyn," George said as they stepped onto the street.

"He was pretty upset. I've noticed him having fits of anger, sometimes bordering on rage, lately," Alicia added.

"I thought it was just me! He is normally so calm and collected. Lately he just seems to be so aggressive, especially when it comes to something that annoys him," George agreed with Alicia.

"He doesn't sleep much anymore either, and yet he seems to have so much energy. I catch him staring out his window some nights," Alicia said, her voice heavy with concern.

"I think I know what it is. He'll be fine, Mrs. Silver. He's just going through some stuff; we both know this isn't his true personality," George said and side hugged Alicia. They made it to the Silver house and Austyn was sitting on the living room couch with his head in his hands.

"Sorry, Mom; sorry, George," Austyn apologized without lifting his head.

"How did you know I was here too?" George asked in surprise.

Austyn looked up and responded, "I could smell you." George and Alicia looked at each other with puzzled expressions and then Austyn continued, "I could also hear you approaching the house."

"Oh, okay…I guess I can be pretty loud sometimes," George responded with an uneasy smile.

"Son, Thomas apologized for his comments. He didn't know that your father was a deputy," Alicia explained.

"I know that, Mom. I heard him apologize when I was leaving, but he got me so mad. It was too late for me to turnaround and pretend everything was okay," Austyn replied, he looked to George and said "George, please tell your folks that I am truly sorry."

"Don't worry about it, Austyn. My folks are good, you know you are their second son. They have your back," George replied and put his hand on Austyn's shoulder.

"Okay, if everything is okay here, I'm going to go back and help with the dishes," Alicia stated and gave both boys a kiss on their cheek.

"Okay, Mom." Austyn returned the kiss. His mother left the house and George closed the door.

"Bro, I need you to be honest with me," George said seriously once Austyn's mom was gone.

"Sure, what's up?" Austyn answered, a bewildered look on his face.

"What are you taking?" George asked.

"What do you mean?" Austyn responded even more confused.

"'Roids, Austyn. It's obvious you're taking steroids!" George shouted at his friend.

"I'm not taking steroids, you dumbass!" Austyn shouted back angrily.

"You're at least twice as strong as before, you have amazing stamina that's come from nowhere, you have been extremely irritated lately, and, honestly, it seems like you're dealing with some roid rage!" George stated.

"I swear on our friendship that I have never touched that crap!" Austyn refuted loudly.

"You need help, Austyn. You need help. Let me help you!" George pleaded with his friend.

"George, you know I would come to you if I needed help with anything. You have always trusted me, why don't you trust me now?!" Austyn replied.

"I…I…I do trust you, bro. I just don't want to see anything happen to you," George said, choking back tears. Austyn saw his friend's concern and walked over to George and pulled him into a hug. "I love you Austyn, you're my brother."

"I love you too, bro," Austyn said, returning the sentiment to his best friend. "But don't get the wrong idea, I'm not gay."

George wiped his tears and the two young men laughed.

George hung out with Austyn for the remainder of the evening. During that time, Austyn received a text message from D apologizing for Thomas and wishing him a Happy Thanksgiving. Austyn responded with an apology of his own and said he would personally apologize to Thomas for his behavior the next time they crossed paths. D sent him a smiley emoji and the words "air hug!" Austyn smiled and returned the "air hug."

During that time, George returned home briefly to bring back a round of second servings of Thanksgiving dinner that the two friends devoured. After playing a few rounds of *Call to Action* and watching the *Revengers* movie, George got up from the gaming chair and said, "I gotta get home. I'm gonna shower and call Emily."

"Alright, sounds good. Surprised you went this long without calling her or vice versa," Austyn replied half-sarcastically.

"Yeah, yeah, whatever dude. Tomorrow you will get to know each other better and you'll understand why I like her so much," George responded with a grin.

"I'm sure I will, bro. Laters." Austyn stood up and the two performed their handshake. Austyn walked George to the door and watched as he crossed the street. He turned around to go back to his room but stopped when the sensation of being watched came over him. It was a feeling he had never felt before, but he knew it was a feeling that he shouldn't ignore. He ran upstairs to the loft, pulled open the window, and carefully stepped onto the roof. He crouched down into a ready-to-pounce position and scanned the area. Austyn saw George entering his house, but other than that and the rustling of the leaves in the wind, everything was still. Austyn had all but given up on finding the source of his uneasiness when he saw a dark figure descending an oak tree. The figure appeared to be fixated on the Bala residence.

Austyn went back inside and ran downstairs. He pushed through the front door, but by the time he made it to the sidewalk, the figure was gone. Austyn didn't know if what he had seen was real or a daydream; his imagination had been running wild over the past three weeks. Even though he wasn't having nightmares, he still found himself seeing things from time to time. Austyn scratched his cheek pensively and returned to his house. He wondered if he should keep what he saw, or at least what he thought he saw, to himself or share it with George. He didn't want to worry him for something that could have been a figment of his imagination.

CHAPTER EIGHT: DRIVE-IN

George was buttoning up the dress shirt that his mother had just bought for him. It was a lime green button-down shirt that was perfectly ironed. His blue jeans were dark and had been ironed as well. His Johnston and Murray brown shoes were being broken in for the first time. George was a little nervous since this was a big night for him. It would be the first time he had seen Emily since the crazy night at Slaughter Creek.

"Looking sharp little man!" D complimented her brother from the doorway. She was getting ready to head to the medical center and was dressed in her usual black scrubs and had her hair up in a bun.

"Thanks, sis. I'm nervous; I think I'm going to meet her dad today." George looked at his sister nervously.

"Just be yourself, you'll be fine!" D encouraged her brother. George took a deep breath and checked his hair in the mirror.

"Aye, que chulo! My handsome baby boy!" Letty gleefully complimented her son as she helped him fix his hair. "This Emily girl better be nice to you!" she said as she pointed at George.

"Mom, she is nice. You'll like her, I promise," George said with a laugh and gently pushed his mother's hand out of his face.

"Okay, I'm leaving, have to beat the traffic," D cut in and gave her mom and brother a kiss on their cheeks.

"Be careful, sis!" George replied.

"Have a good day at work, mija." Letty returned the kiss to her daughter.

D ran downstairs and grabbed the car keys off the key holder. She heard the back door open and turned around to see Austyn looking back at her. He was wearing a deep navy blue polo shirt and tan pants with blue shoes. D opened her eyes in wide surprise at Austyn's unexpected appearance. While she stared at him longer than she meant to, she couldn't help thinking how good he looked.

"Hi Damaris!" Austyn said with a smile.

D blinked, coming back to herself. "H-hi Austyn," she stuttered. "I've got to get going. You two be safe tonight, and have fun," she said before giving him a hug goodbye. She could smell his cologne and aftershave and wanted to stay in the hug a little longer but didn't want to send any mixed signals. She looked up at Austyn and smiled before she walked out of the kitchen and left the house.

Austyn watched D leave and was amazed that even when she wasn't trying, she was beautiful and smelled like a flower that was picked from the Garden of Eden itself. He went upstairs to George's room to find Letty fixing George's pant leg over the tongue of his shoe.

"Hi, Austyn. My, you look very handsome," Letty said adoringly.

"Hello, Mrs. Bala, thank you. I'm nothing compared to you! You always look beautiful ma'am," Austyn replied to a smiling Letty.

"What up Austyn! We look good, bro! Let's go!" George said and motioned for Austyn to stand next to him in front of the mirror.

"Oh, you two are so handsome. Let me take a picture!" Letty asked and grabbed George's cell phone.

"Okay, Mom, do you know how to get to the camera?" George replied as he posed with Austyn.

"Yes, I know what I'm doing," Letty replied and held the phone up to her face. "Hold still and smile boys." Letty snapped multiple pictures and reviewed them to make sure they came out good. "Be sure to text me the pictures, mijo," she said and handed George back his phone.

"I will, Mom." George answered and looked at the pictures. Letty hugged the boys and left the room with one last request for them to be careful.

George and Austyn went down the stairs into the living room where George Sr. was watching TV. George stood next to his dad and said, "We're leaving, dad."

"Okay, son," George Sr. reached into his pant pocket and gave George the keys to the truck. "Remember, you break my truck, I break your ass," he added with a grin. "Both of you."

"Got it, dad!" George replied and hugged his dad.

"Yes, sir!" Austyn responded and shook George Sr.'s hand.

"Seriously, have fun boys, but be safe. For God's sake call if you are going to be running late. You know mom will have us up waiting all night until you get home," George Sr. pleaded with the boys.

"Will do, Dad." George tossed the keys in his hand and told Austyn, "Let's fly!" The friends jumped in the truck and got on the road, heading to the north part of San Antonio to pick up Emily.

They pulled up to a tan-colored two-story house. George went to the door and met Emily's parents, and although it was nerve-racking for him, it went about as good as it could have gone.

They left the house that Emily had to be home before her midnight curfew imposed by her dad. George walked her to the passenger side of the freshly-washed, shiny black truck. He opened the door for her and helped her into the vehicle. Austyn, still waiting in the truck, greeted Emily with a handshake from the backseat. The three left Emily's neighborhood and got on the road for the twenty-five minute drive up to New Braunfels to pick up Olivia.

On the drive, they chatted about the movie they were going to see, and the fact the Emily had never been to a drive-in before. Then, Emily remembered that she had something to share with George.

"Remember when you asked me to see if my cousin heard anything about the dead body that they found at the creek?"

"Yeah, did she hear anything?" George asked curiously.

Austyn moved to the edge of his seat in the middle of the rear bench, and leaned in.

"Yes. Sarah started dating this guy she met at a club, and it turns out that his dad is a homicide detective for Travis County," Emily replied.

"Really? That's interesting," George remarked, glancing at the GPS he was following to find Olivia's house.

"Well, she asked him about the dead guy. His dad was one of the detectives assigned to the case," Emily continued.

"What a coincidence," Austyn added.

"Right! Anyway, he said that the dead guy was probably a French tourist, and possibly a nudist. Obviously, he had no identification on him, but he had tattoos that were all in French. They have no leads but there something else that the detectives found puzzling. The medical examiner said that the bullets that were used to murder him were pure silver!" Emily finished excitedly, explaining what she had learned from her cousin.

"That's so strange," George replied.

Austyn sat back and thought about what Emily had just revealed, and although he did think the silver bullets were an interesting piece of information, he couldn't get past the fact that the dead guy was French. "Vous êtes le prochain!" The words from his nightmare rang in his head on repeat. *How the hell did my nightmare know to include the fact that the man was French?* Austyn wondered. *What could the nightmare have possibly meant?* Thoughts raced uncontrollably through his mind but none of them made sense.

"Austy! You still with us?" George asked while waving his hand in front of Austyn's face.

"Yeah, sorry. I was just thinking," Austyn replied.

"Looked like you were daydreaming," George said, bringing the truck to a stop. "We're here dude, go get Olivia." George said, shooing Austyn out of the truck.

Though feeling out of sorts, Austyn gathered himself and climbed out of the truck.

Emily looked at George, confused. George looked at Austyn's retreating form and said, "He's had a long day. I think he's a little tired." They both giggled and turned to watch Austyn standing at the door talking to an older couple who were presumably Olivia's parents. Olivia appeared and stepped outside, and Austyn shook the her parents' hands.

As he walked Olivia to the truck, he happened to look over his left shoulder. He saw an older black van driving down the street in their direction. As the van passed the truck, the driver, a man with long, dark stringy hair, glared pointedly at Austyn.

The van vanished over the hill at the end of the block, but Austyn kept an eye out for it as he helped Olivia into the truck. He had a bad feeling about the van. He watched for a few more seconds but it seemed to be gone now, and no one else seemed to have noticed it let alone be worried about it.

When she got in the truck, Olivia greeted Emily and George happily, and they headed off to the drive-in. Austyn was still feeling distracted by the information that Emily had given them, and he couldn't seem to shake the feeling of uneasiness he had gotten from the man in the black van. Olivia was making conversation with him, and he was feigning interest, but he was having a hard time focusing on what she was saying.

"Well, what do you think?" Olivia asked, waiting for a response.

"Uh...I'm sorry...can you repeat that?" Austyn asked.

"Austyn, you silly nut. I asked if you wanted to come over to my house tomorrow for a barbeque!" Olivia repeated her question with a laugh.

"Oh...I don—" Austyn started, but he was cut off by George.

"Yes! We will be there. What time?"

"Perfect! Four o'clock. It's going to be so much fun, and my dad is a great griller!" Olivia said happily. Austyn didn't say a word; instead, he nodded in agreement and forced a smile onto his face.

The truck eventually slowed to a halt and the foursome found themselves in line to enter the "Star-Spangled Drive-In Theatre" complex. The tickets were purchased, and George found the perfect parking spot. It wasn't so close that they might not be able to see the whole screen at once, yet it wasn't so far away that the background behind the screen would be a distraction during the movie.

"This is a great spot!" Emily stated elatedly.

"Thanks! My dad always said that the trick to the drive-in is to find what he calls the 'sweet spot,'" George replied. He had parked reversed so that they could set up in the bed of the truck with a Bluetooth FM radio speaker.

"We're gonna grab popcorn and drinks before the movie starts. Would you like something?" Austyn asked the girls as he jumped off the truck. He took their orders and headed off to the concession but stopped and waited for George to catch up to him.

"Dude, why did you say yes about tomorrow?" Austyn hissed, giving George a look of annoyance.

"Because you need a distraction with all that has been going on with you lately. Besides, it gives me another chance to see Emily," George said with a smirk.

"Ass!" Austyn replied and slugged George on the arm jokingly.

"Damn Austyn! That one really hurt!" George winced and grabbed his left arm. They arm slugged each other regularly but never with the intent of doing real damage. They laughed and walked into the concession stand, George still rubbing his arm.

"What Emily said freaked me out," Austyn said, abruptly changing the subject.

"It was strange. Who uses silver bullets to kill someone?" George replied.

"I'm more freaked out that the dude was French," Austyn added before they placed their order for popcorn, pizza, nachos, candy, and soda at the counter. The concession worker turned and started to put the order together.

"Why did that freak you out?" George asked curiously.

"Because in my nightmare," Austyn looked around and lowered his voice so only George could hear him, "the guy spoke to me in French."

"I thought you didn't know what language it was?" asked George.

"I didn't, but when I told D about my nightmare she told me that it was French for *"You're next,"* Austyn stated. Their order was slid to them across the counter and Austyn paid for everything. The two grabbed the snacks and headed back to the truck.

"That's freaky! How did your dream know he was French?" George was perplexed by the idea.

"That's what's freaking me out! I don't know!" Austyn replied anxiously.

"Maybe we are making too big a deal out of this. It probably has more to do with intuition than anything else," George replied.

"Excuse me, Dr. Bala," Austyn responded jokingly. They made it back to the truck where Emily and Olivia had already set up the seating arrangements. George and Austyn passed out the snacks and took their respective spots.

The night was filled with screams and jeers and demonic clowns terrorizing the group of college kids that visited the amusement park. Just like the night at the Slaughter Creek House of Terror, Emily had jumped into George's embrace several times throughout the night. Olivia had gotten close to Austyn and both of her hands were wrapped around his left arm. When something scary happened on screen, she would turn and bury her face into his shoulder. Austyn was doing his best not to lead her on, but he also didn't want to dismiss her or hurt her feelings.

Austyn normally enjoyed a scary movie, but he was extremely jittery and preoccupied all night. He noticed that the moon was out and bright, though not quite full. He turned back to where George and Emily were sitting and saw Emily feeding popcorn to George, and George feeding nachos to Emily. He rolled his eyes and continued to watch the movie. Olivia had to use the restroom, so Austyn escorted her to give George and Emily some time alone.

"The movie is really scary, huh?" Olivia asked Austyn.

"Yeah, it has its moments," Austyn replied.

"Did I do something wrong Austyn?" Olivia asked quietly.

"No, why would you think that?" Austyn responded.

"It just seems like you're ignoring me, and you don't look happy to be here," she explained. Austyn ran a hand over his face and took a deep breath.

"Olivia, nothing is wrong. I just have a lot on my mind right now. I am having a good time here with you, I apologize for making you feel like that," Austyn responded and held his bent arm out for her to hold as he walked her. He really did feel bad for making Olivia feel ignored. She smiled and grabbed his arm. Austyn waited outside the women's restroom for Olivia to come out, and while he was waiting, he heard loud screams coming from their theatre. He peaked out around the corner to see try and see the screen. When he did, he noticed a black van parked behind and catty-corner to where George's truck was parked. He was about to get a better look, when the restroom door opened and Olivia popped out.

"Sorry I made you wait. Had to freshen up a little," Olivia apologized.

"No worries," Austyn said quickly before returning his attention to the theatre lot. The van was gone. He was sure that it had been there, and it appeared to be the same van that he had seen on Olivia's street.

"Is everything okay?" Olivia asked, looking in the direction Austyn was staring. Austyn turned back to look at her and smiled. He didn't want to scare Olivia, although he was certain it was the same van from earlier, there was always the possibility that he was mistaken.

"Yeah, I thought I saw something, but it was nothing. Ready to go back?" he asked, extending his arm again. Olivia took his arm and they walked back to the truck.

The movie ended on a cliffhanger that insinuated a sequel and maybe even a prequel would be following. On the way home, the group stopped at a Texas Burger restaurant to eat. They laughed and had a good time, and Austyn found himself loosening up and was even beginning to warm up to Olivia.

It was just past ten o'clock and George wanted to make sure he got Emily back before her curfew out of respect for her dad. His dad had always told him that when he dates someone and the parents give a curfew, do your best to beat it by at least an hour.

Before dropping Emily off, they stopped to drop off Olivia, and Austyn walked her to her door.

"So, I'll see you tomorrow?" Olivia asked hopefully.

"Yes, I'll be here around four o'clock," Austyn confirmed. Olivia smiled and gave him a big hug before she entered her house. Austyn returned to the truck and George and Emily were giggling.

"What?" he asked the two poster children for PDA.

"That was a nice, tight hug there, bro," George replied.

"It sure was," Emily agreed, barely containing another giggle.

"Just drive," Austyn said, and he put his hands behind his head. He was still feeling antsy, and he didn't know why.

It was almost eleven, and they had finally arrived at Emily's house. George ran to Emily's side to open the truck door for her and helped her down. He walked her to her porch and when they got to the door he said, "I hope you had a good time."

"I did! It was a fun night. Can't wait to do it again!" Emily responded.

"Pick you up tomorrow around 3:30?" George asked with regard to Olivia's barbeque invite.

"For sure, I'll be ready," Emily answered with a smile. She looked into George's eyes and then looked down at her feet. George was nervous, but he knew that the night had gone well, and that Emily liked him. He took a breath and caressed her face with both hands. She looked up at him and closed her eyes, he leaned forward, and they embraced in a soft kiss.

Austyn was watching from the truck and recording everything on his phone. He figured he had to repay George for Emily making fun of him, volunteering him to help with the attic shores, and for making plans for him with Olivia. It would be fun to show Mr. and Mrs. Bala, and D, for that matter.

Emily's father had come to the door after Emily had gone inside and called George back to the porch. George had begun to sweat and could feel his face flush red. He was sure that her father had seen him kiss his daughter and was going to unleash the hounds of hell on him.

"I just wanted to tell you that I really appreciate you taking care of my

Emmy and bringing her home safe. Thank you," Emily's dad said and reached his hand out to offer a respectful handshake.

"Um...yes, sir! Th...Thank you for allowing me to take your daughter out tonight, sir!" George responded and shook his hand. Emily had told him her last name during their conversations, and he was even following her on social media, but for the life of him he could not remember her last name or how to address her father as anything other than sir. Even with the memory lapse, George was ecstatic! He couldn't believe that he had already earned respect points with Emily's dad. He was going to make sure to thank his dad for the dating advice and his mom for showing him proper etiquette and how to treat a girl with respect. He jumped into the truck and screamed, "HELL YEAH!!!"

He was dancing in place and pumping his fist, all the while Austyn was still recording. But George didn't care, he was on cloud nine.

CHAPTER NINE: ABDUCTED

Laughter was ringing through the Bala house. George Sr. was in tears watching his son nearly pee his pants when Emily's dad called him back to the porch. The Bala family was gathered around Austyn's phone as he replayed the kiss goodnight between George and Emily.

"Way to go, lil' man!" D laughed and slapped George's shoulder.

"Georgie, you should have waited to kiss her. Why didn't you wait?" Letty asked with a hint of admonishment.

"Mom…I…but…" George stuttered. He was embarrassed and was being roasted from all sides.

"That's my boy!" George Sr. said jokingly. Letty didn't find her husband's comments very amusing and gave him a disapproving stare.

"Thanks, Dad," George responded.

"And you're going to see this Emily girl again today?" Letty asked worriedly.

"Yes mother. I told you, we are going to a barbecue that Austyn's girlfriend Olivia invited us to," George replied, trying to drag Austyn into the crossfire.

"Eh, eh, eh…not my girlfriend. Just a friend," Austyn inserted while the footage continued playing.

"Oookay…we need to go now," George said trying to escape the grips of his family and the questions from his mom. Austyn looked at his watch and agreed. He had embarrassed his friend enough for one day. He stopped the video and promised to keep it on his phone so he could replay it for them any time.

"Austyn, I need you to send me that video," Letty demanded jokingly.

"Yes, ma'am!"

"Dude, you better delete it!" George shouted back at his friend.

"Georgie, be smart, son. I'm too young to be a grandma!" Letty shouted out the front door as George and Austyn got into Austyn's Firebird.

"Really?!" George shouted at Austyn. Austyn couldn't help himself and he exploded with laughter, tears rolling down his cheeks. George caved in and joined in the laughter; he knew that he would do the same to Austyn if the shoe were on the other foot. George broke the laughter and added in a serious tone, "Seriously, though, don't send that to my mom."

Austyn, still laughing, turned the Firebird on and looked to George and said, "Hold on to your juevos!" Austyn revved his engine and the Firebird raced down the street. They stopped to pick up Emily from her house and continued the trip to Olivia's, neither of them mentioning the video that Austyn had captured.

George had switched to the back seat to sit with Emily and while the two were talking it up, Austyn couldn't help but feel like a chauffeur. He rolled his eyes at his friend and turned his music up a bit. He glanced at his rearview mirror and caught a glimpse of what he thought was a black van. His head swiveled on his shoulders as he scanned all the mirrors, but he didn't see it. The black van was starting to become a worry for Austyn. Either it was real and someone is following him, or it was his imagination and he needed to deal with a whole different kind of problem.

The Firebird parked next to the curb in front of Olivia's house. Olivia was already standing in the entryway to her house, waving at them as they parked.

"Hi everyone!" Olivia greeted everyone while they were getting out of the car.

"Hello!" replied George while he was helping Emily out from the backseat.

"Hi Liv!" Emily replied happily and waved.

Austyn walked up to Olivia and gave her a hello hug and said, "Hi."

Olivia led the group through the house to the covered backyard patio where a table for eight was set up under the fan. Olivia then Austyn and George to her parents, the Carvajals.

George and Austyn accompanied Mr. Carvajal to the grill to conversate.

Inside a large kennel nearby, a large German shepherd, Copper, was leaning up on his hind legs on the kennel door. He was barking relentlessly at the visitors.

"Copper! Quiet down!" Mr. Carvajal shouted at the barking dog. Copper ignored the commands and continued barking. Mr. Carvajal continued shouting at the dog, but to no avail. He turned to George and Austyn and said, "Apologies, boys. He is never like this. He is usually friendly with everyone."

"It's no problem, Mr. Carvajal. My husky has her moments from time to time," George replied.

"He is a beautiful dog, sir," Austyn added, staring at the barking dog. He asked Mr. Carvajal, "Do you mind if I go and talk to him?"

"Be my guest," Mr. Carvajal responded, motioning with an arm toward the kennel.

As Austyn approached, Copper reared back against the opposite kennel wall and barked more aggressively. Austyn crouched down so he was at eyelevel with Copper, and said in a low grumble, "Stop!" Austyn's nostrils were flared and his lips were curled, exposing his canines. Copper whimpered and submissively laid on the ground and immediately stopped barking. Austyn smiled and said, "Thank you!" He got up and walked back to the grill. George and Mr. Carvajal were staring at him in complete surprise.

"Impressive, young man," Mr. Carvajal complimented Austyn.

"That was different," George commented to no one in particular.

"Thank you, sir. I think he just needed to get a better look at me and catch my scent," Austyn responded.

"Whatever it was, it worked. Now! Let's go and enjoy these ribeye steaks!" Mr. Carvajal enthusiastically said, and he removed the perfectly cooked steaks from the grill and placed them on a tray. The three men met the waiting ladies at the patio table. The food was laid out on top of a smaller table, buffet style. They served themselves and sat down to enjoy a nice Sunday meal.

The barbeque was pleasant, and Mr. and Mrs. Carvajal were nice people who made their guests feel welcomed. They had questions for the three the visitors, but they focused the majority of those questions on Austyn. When all was said and done, the steaks were gone, and the sun was setting. The once blue sky was now painted with hints of orange and purple.

The Carvajals went inside their house to start washing dishes and to give the young adults some time to themselves. George and Emily were sitting close and were engaged in deep conversation. Olivia and Austyn were sitting with their feet in the Carvajal's in-ground swimming pool.

"This is a beautiful pool," Austyn said to Olivia.

"Thank you. Maybe when it is warmer, we can go for a swim," she replied.

"Sure," Austyn answered. He felt Olivia grab his hand and interlock her fingers into his. He was overcome with guilt; he had done his best not to lead her on up to that point. He was about to tell her that he only wanted to be friends, but that's when the moonlight broke through the clouds and shone down on them. Austyn felt a sensational burst of aggression from deep within. He looked up at the moon and tried to understand where this feeling was coming from and exactly what it was. Copper suddenly jumped up and began barking again. Olivia turned to her dog and tried to silence him. Austyn looked down at his hand interlocked with Olivia's. She turned back to face him, smiling innocently, and he leaned forward and kissed her passionately. In his mind he knew that he should stop, but he couldn't.

After the long bout of making out, they parted their lips from each other. Olivia looked into Austyn's eyes with an expression of euphoria. She smiled at him, caressed his face with her right hand, and said, "Wow! That was incredible. I was even seeing things."

"It was nice, I would like to do it again," Austyn replied. He was amped up, he could feel his heart pounding and the hairs on his body were standing on end. Every one of his senses were keenly aware of his surroundings. The aggression was growing within him, and his better judgement could not compete with what he was feeling. He could hear Olivia's heartbeat, smell the release of her pheromones, and could taste her lips while they were kissing. He stood up and lifted her with his hand. He looked around the garden and guided her behind the shed in the corner of the yard. They went around the corner of the small shed, hidden from view of the patio, and Austyn began kissing Olivia again, deeper and more passionately this time. He wanted more. He took her to the ground and was straddled on top of her. Olivia was breathing heavily and staring into Austyn's eyes. She held her breath and Austyn went in for another kiss.

"My parents," Olivia whispered.

"They are still washing dishes, don't worry," Austyn whispered back.

"How do you know?" Olivia asked softly.

"I can hear them," Austyn replied. He was moving closer slowly and was running his hands through her hair. He stopped when he saw Olivia gasp. "What's wrong?"

"Nothing, I think it is just the excitement of the moment. For a second there, I swear your eyes were yellow," Olivia added with a playful giggle.

Thoughts of the yellow eyes from his nightmares of the Slaughter Creek House of Terror and the naked man with yellow eyes at the creek flooded his mind. He snapped out of what felt like an aphrodisiac-induced trance. He jumped up off Olivia and said, "I'm so sorry, Olivia!"

"Wh..Sorry for what?" asked a confused Olivia leaning up on her forearms.

"I have to go!" Austyn said and rushed back to where George and Emily were sitting. Olivia stayed where she was, completely dumbfounded by what had just happened.

"What's up, bro?" George asked when he saw Austyn's uneasy expression.

"Is he alright?" Emily whispered into George's ear.

"No, I'm not alright. I don't feel well. We need to leave. Now!" Austyn answered Emily to her surprise and walked through the backyard gate into the front yard. Olivia stormed out from around the corner of the shed.

"Liv, so sorry. We have to go. I'll call you later," Emily apologized.

"Sorry Olivia, I think Austyn isn't feeling well. Please thank your parents for the wonderful time," George added. He grabbed Emily's hand and they went around to the front yard.

Austyn was standing next to his car. Arms extended and hands pressed firmly on the car's red hood. He could hear George and Emily getting closer, he turned and tossed George his keys and said, "Here, I can't drive."

"Alright, bro," George replied with concern.

George opened the passenger door and folded the seat forward so Austyn could get in. He helped Emily into the front seat and closed the door. George started the car and proceeded to drive Emily home. It was a quiet ride; Austyn kept looking at his eyes in the rearview mirror from the back seat, checking for anything glowing of yellow. George and Emily kept their conversation to small talk, and saying very little to Austyn.

They made it to Emily's house after a thirty-minute drive that felt like thirty hours. George opened the car door and held Emily's hand as she exited the Firebird.

"Bye Austyn, hope you feel better," Emily said and waved to Austyn.

"Bye Emily, thanks," Austyn responded. George held Emily's hand and walked her to her door.

"I know it was short, but I really enjoyed being with you today. Just wish it was for a little longer," George said to Emily, holding both of her hands.

"Me too, but it's okay. I'm sure we will have more chances to see each other. Austyn looks like he needs you right now," Emily replied. George was pleased with how understanding Emily was; to this point, she was everything that he had been praying for in a girl. He pulled Emily towards him with a hug and gave her a warm goodnight kiss before she went inside.

George sat down back in the driver's seat of the Firebird. Austyn had jumped to the front passenger seat.

"You are seriously starting to freak me out, Austyn," George said with sincerity.

"You don't understand what I am going through," Austyn replied.

"Well help me understand, bro! I saw you having a good time with Olivia, and then you took her behind the shed. Everything was fine."

"I can't explain it, the way I was feeling inside. The aggression, the rage, the horniness. I was close to taking it all the way with her, I couldn't control myself!" Austyn tried to explain.

"Then, did y'all…?" George asked, turning his eyes back to the road. He looked down at the gauges and the fuel warning was lit.

"No. We didn't," Austyn replied with his head resting back against the headrest.

"Why did you stop?" George asked confusedly. He saw a gas station at the next exit and signaled to exit.

"She...she...said my eyes were yellow," Austyn said staring at George.

George was surprised and turned to look into Austyn's eyes; they weren't yellow, but there was something missing. The light that Austyn always seemed to have was gone. George frowned and faced forward again. He remembered all the times Austyn had mentioned seeing yellow eyes in his nightmares.

"I'm gonna get some gas," George said and stopped the Firebird next to gas pump number three of the Fast Trip gas station. Austyn reached into his back pocket to pull out his wallet to pay for the gas and George stopped him. "No, don't worry, bro. I got it."

"Thanks, bro. I'm gonna use the restroom," Austyn replied and got out of the car. He walked into the gas station and found the men's restroom. While George was pumping the gas, a black van pulled up to the gas pump on the opposite side of the Firebird.

The clank of the pump nozzle stopping because of the full gas tank rang. George pulled the nozzle from the gas tank and shook it a few times to get the last few drops of gas to fall into the tank. As he turned to put the nozzle back on the pump, he was grabbed from behind and a rag was forcibly placed over his nose and mouth. George fell limp into the arms of his unknown assailant dressed in black tactical clothing. George was dragged to the van and tossed into the open sliding doorway. As the attacker slid the door closed, he glanced into the store and met Austyn's eyes.

Austyn was looking out towards the gas pump through the glass walls of the building watching the mysterious man drag George into the same black van that he had seen driving down Olivia's street, at the drive-in, and following them on the highway earlier that day. The man jumped in the van and sped away from the gas station.

Austyn ran out the gas station doors and saw that the gas pump nozzle was thrown on the ground and the Firebird's gas cap had not been replaced. Austyn put the gas cap back on and burned out in the same direction the van had gone. Austyn was weaving in and out of traffic trying to catch up to the black van, pushing his speedometer past the 120 miles per hour mark. After a couple of minutes of reckless driving, Austyn realized it was hopeless. He had lost the van. He didn't know what else to do, so he called the police and returned to the gas station to wait for a Bexar County Deputy to arrive.

CHAPTER TEN: THE NAME IS LOGAN

A fly that was buzzing around and continuously landing and taking off for flight was hovering around an unconscious George's head. He was laying face up with his back on a dirt floor littered with hay. The rays of sunlight were filtering in through the cracks and crevices of the wooden structure surrounding him and they were dancing on his face. George began to open his eyes and he squinted to try to put in to focus the blurry scenery around him. He struggled to get to his feet, and when he finally was able to stand, he held his hands against the sides of his head, feeling lightheaded and dizzy.

A blast of sunlight rushed into the room and the brilliant flash blinded George for a moment. He held his left hand out in front of his face, shielding his eyes from the direction of the light. He was able to make out blurry shapes and he could see a figure dressed in black closing a large door and shutting out the light. George blinked rapidly as his eyes adjusted to the low light once again. He saw the man dressed in black tactical garb climbing a ladder that stretched from the ground to a second level where he lost sight of him. George realized he must be in a barn.

George focused his attention to his immediate surroundings. He was encircled by a heavy-duty iron cage. He was locked up like an animal; a prisoner of an unknown captor. He shook the iron bars to test their sturdiness; they did not have much give. He stared up to the level above waiting for the figure to reappear. When the man did not reappear, he shouted, "Hey! Let me out of here!" After no response George began to yell "Help!"

"Yell all you wish. No one can hear you," said the unseen abductor, his European accent obvious.

"Why are you doing this?!" George shouted angrily. The unknown man said nothing.

Hours had passed and George realized that what he had been told about screaming for help was true. No one was coming because no one could hear him. He crept back into the far corner of the cell and sat with his knees bent up against the post. He was scared and confused. *Why am I here? Who is this guy? Where am I? My family is going to be so worried. I am going to die here.* Though he tried not to, he couldn't help but shed tears. The drops ran down his cheeks as he reflected on his life, his friends, and his family.

The thumps of heavy boots thudded against the second level floor. The abductor in black was visible once again, looking down at the iron cell, seeing George sitting in the corner. He chuckled and descended the ladder.

"I didn't think your kind had the capacity to cry."

George looked up at the monster in black and shouted, "Screw you, you psychotic sack of shit! You don't know anything about me!"

"Hmm, don't know anything about you? I know more about you than you know about yourself!" the stoutly built stranger shouted. "Ce soir vient la pleine lune," he mumbled to himself. He then turned and walked away from the cage.

"You're crazy, man! I've never seen you before in my life!" George replied.

The stranger stopped dead in his tracks, looked back at George and said, "But I've seen you!" He turned his head forward and walked out of the building, leaving George riddled with confusion and fear.

The man went to his van and opened the back doors and rooted through the weapons, gadgets, and tools loaded in the vehicle. He had a small arsenal that included daggers, ammunition, flash grenades, and a couple of handguns. He grabbed a tripod and a small tablet that was underneath cables and zip ties, and shut the door. He looked at his watch. It was a quarter until two in the afternoon; he gazed into the sky and searched the horizon. The rural landscape was enclosed by a barbed wire fence. The man leaned back against the sliding door of the van, took a deep breath, looked up and said to himself,

"Seigneur, pardonne-moi ce que je vais faire." He placed his hands together and whispered a prayer in French. When he completed his prayer, made the sign of the cross and kissed his crucifix necklace. The stranger turned his attention to the abandoned, beat up barn and stared at it.

Inside the barn George was pacing around, trying to think of ways to get out of the cage. He had seen so many movies about people being kidnapped or held prisoner in some type of cage or room and thought of all the ways they had tried to escape to come up with something. In his mind, when he watched those movies, he had always said that if he wherever in that predicament, he would find a way out. Now was his chance. The barn door opened, and the stranger walked in.

The man set up the tripod with a camera facing the cage. He rolled out a table and placed a duffel bag on the ground. He reached into the bag while a scared and confused George looked on. The stranger placed a nickel-plated handgun on the table, an empty fifteen-round magazine, a box of ammunition, and a small clear bottle of liquid with a cross embossed across the face.

"Dude what kind of a freak are you?!" George asked in a bewildered tone.

"I am not a *freak*, as you put it. I am doing my sworn duty; one that has been passed down in my family from generation to generation," the stranger explained calmly.

"So, your whole family is nuts?!" George yelled angrily at the stranger.

"Do not speak ill off my family you monster. For centuries, my family has protected the world from the evil that creeps in the moonlight. My forefathers, my cousins, and my brothers have all sacrificed themselves for who you used to be, and for your family," the stranger replied with an upset tone.

"Protect the world from evil?! You need help, man! What you are doing right now is evil. It looks like you're getting ready to sacrifice me for some kind of twisted satanic ritual or something!" George retorted.

"I am not evil, and I am truly sorry for what I must do tonight, George," The stranger replied staring into George's eyes.

"How do you know my name? Who the hell are you?!" George shouted. The stranger walked around the table upon which sat the weaponry he had laid out, and he approached the cage. He was holding a silver bullet between his thumb and pointer finger in front of him.

"My name is Jean Logano Bergier. Logan for short," Logan answered.

"Logan?" George repeated.

"Yes, the name is Logan," he affirmed.

George stared at Logan who was still standing in front of the cage and then looked past him to table that was set up with the gun and ammunition. He refocused on Logan and asked, "Are you going to kill me?"

"Unfortunately, I must," Logan responded with a sigh.

"Why? My family? Emily? What did I do to deserve this?" George pleaded with tears in his eyes.

"Believe me, George, tonight I will be doing you, your family, and Emily a favor," Logan replied sympathetically.

"Logan, how are you doing me a favor if you are going to murder me?" George responded sadly.

"I shall free you of the curse that was wrongfully passed on to you," answered Logan.

"Curse? What curse, Logan?!" George asked anxiously.

"The curse of the full moon, George. The curse of the lycanthrope, a werewolf," Logan explained.

"A werewolf?! You need help, Logan! There is no such thing as a werewolf!" George answered outraged.

"Over two hundred and fifty years ago, in the province of Gevaudan in the Margeride Mountains of south-central France, a string of horrific and gruesome murders began. At first, the people of Gevaudan believed a lunatic was wreaking havoc on the innocent citizens. But the bodies were found dismembered and partially eaten, so the theory was that an animal of some sort was responsible, possibly a wolf."

George listened as Logan spun his tale, still trying to wrap his mind around the concept.

Logan continued the story. "That is until one day a witness saw a beast that looked to be half a man and half a wolf, but larger than both. This beast was devouring a small child. Many men, women, and children fell prey to this ferocious predator. While the true number of victims is not known, the count on record is 564, though, my family believes the number to be over one thousand.

"During this dark time in the history of France, the Catholic church of Notre Dame called upon descendants of the Crusaders. They called on the family Bergier, to put together a group of hunter-soldiers to learn as much as they could about the beast, and train to cleanse it from this Earth. These new crusaders were called the *Guard of Notre Dame*, and they learned quite a bit in their hunt for the beast of Gevaudan. It quickly became clear that the beast hunted when the moon was full for four days, and they found that they could not kill the beast with ordinary weapons. On one of their hunts for the beast, my great-grandfather's forefather Tumas Logano Bergier, found himself cornered by the beast; it lunged at him and tried to take a bite out of his throat. The jaws of this evil beast bit down on the crucifix of pure silver he was wearing around his neck. The beast swallowed the crucifix and subsequently died. To the surprise of Tumas, the beast transformed in front of his very eyes into a young man. My ancestors believed that the beast was dead, that the killings were over, and that they had won, but the very next day twelve more victims were ravaged. It was then, when the Guard of Notre Dame also learned that the beast had the ability to spread its curse by infecting the blood of innocent victims with a bite. They called this cursed species loup-garou, the werewolf."

"You cannot be serious. Werewolves are real?!" George interrupted in disbelief.

"I am dead serious, George," Logan replied. He walked back to the table and picked up a single round of ammunition and held it up into a single beam of light. It was a silver bullet with a brilliant shine. Logan was pinching it between his thumb and pointer finger, and he approached the cage holding it out in front of him. He continued the story. "The pure silver content of Tumas's crucifix sanitized the blood of the beast. The Guard began constructing weapons coated with pure silver; blades, arrows, and ammunition. The scourge was purged from Gevaudan by the Guard of Notre Dame after three years of plaguing the province. The Guard of Notre

Dame was kept hidden from the public and charged by Pope Clement XIII to vanquish the curse from the Earth. And so, for generations, that is what we have done."

"If this stuff is real, then why haven't we heard of it? Something like this would have been all over the news for centuries!" George stated with frustration.

"For the same reason the world governments keep hidden the truth about extraterrestrial beings. It is convenient and it prevents widespread panic and paranoia. The Catholic church kept the legend from being nothing more than that. A legend. They refuted any evidence that was ever brought to the public eye with claims of heresy, lunacy, or hoaxes. The people, having an unquestioned loyalty to the Vatican, never gave credence to any of the claims. You have heard of several gruesome animal attacks, but they are usually accredited to the local top of the food chain predator." Logan replied.

"How many of these *werewolves* have you killed?" George asked apprehensively.

"Too many to count," Logan answered.

"And when these werewolves are killed, do they not change back to their human form? No one questions the manner of death?" George asked curiously.

"We are usually able to cremate the body and bury the remnants, so that they are never found. These cases are usually filed as missing persons by law enforcement. Every now and then there are witnesses and the police are called, not affording us enough time to properly dispose of the body; hence, they become unsolved murders."

"Fine, Logan. Let's just say for a second that this stuff is true. Why do you think that I am cursed?" George asked Logan worriedly.

"The night before Halloween, at the creek; you were bitten by a werewolf," Logan said, as if confused that George even had to ask. "I was not able to get to you in time, I am terribly sorry. But the curse has been passed on to you, and it is my duty to purify your blood."

"Purify my blood…by killing me?! This is crazy…I wasn't attacked by anyth—" George stopped in the middle of his response when he suddenly remembered what had happened that night at Slaughter Creek. He was in the middle of a conversation with Emily when gunshots rang out in the air. He remembered the chaos that ensued and grabbing D, but not being able to find Austyn. Then Austyn had suddenly appeared and was yelling at them to run. He and his sister made it to the truck and waited for Austyn. There was another gunshot and shortly afterwards, Austyn was running up the trailhead and had jumped into the truck. He looked to Logan and realized that he must have been the shooter at the creek. "It was you! You were the maniac shooting at everybody that night!"

"I am no maniac. I was hunting the loup-garou, my brother Anton and I had been on his trail for months. We thought we had him in Baton Rouge, but he was extremely powerful. Louis Henrie Delacroix. He was different than many others. He enjoyed being the beast and gorging himself on the blood and flesh of the innocent. We had always thought of the afflicted as mindless creatures acting on their primal instincts. We had no reason to think anything different. Until we ran across Delacroix.

"We learned that he was willfully spreading his curse. In doing so, he created a pack of rabid beasts that he was able to command as their alpha. Having the pack not only gave him strength in numbers, but it strengthened his will and the loup-garou within. Anton and I tracked them down and we dispatched the pack. All that was left was Delacroix, and we had him blocked in. We were set to end his reign of terror. But, before we could make our move to put an end to this curse once and for all, out of the shadows emerged a new beast, a new pack member of whom we had not been aware. This creature attacked my brother. While I was able to put down the vile beast, it was too late. Anton was dead and Louis Henrie had escaped. I buried my brother, but I had no time to mourn. I tracked Delacroix to Texas and caught up to him at Slaughter Creek. He was about to devour a transient on the side of the road when I found him. I attacked him and he ran into the woods. When I heard the sounds of revelry from the group of young people, I feared for your lives. I tried desperately to get to him before he got to you. I saw you trip, and as you tried to get up, he bit your leg. I was too late, but I knew that I had to finish the job. I spent five silver bullets blessed by the Pope to put down Delacroix.

"I ran up the trail and I saw you drive away in the black truck, so I took down your license plate."

"But I didn't get..." George trailed off again. He realized that if what Logan was saying was true, he wasn't the one Logan was looking for. It was Austyn. George now had a dilemma; if he told Logan that Austyn was the one that was attacked that night, Austyn would then certainly become the target. But he wondered how any of this could be true. It was outrageous. Logan was delusional. *Why is he waiting so long to kill me if he's so sure I was the one bitten?* George decided that the best move at the moment was to keep him talking. Maybe there was a chance that the compassionate side of Logan would realize that he was dealing with a real person and not some mythical creature. "Why don't you get it over with and end it already? What are you waiting for?" George asked.

Logan walked away from the cage and placed the silver bullet he was holding on the table. He stood fourteen more rounds upright, so that they were aligned in three rows of five. "I am not a murderer, George. You are not the target; it is the beast festering within that will reveal itself tonight. I will sit here with you, feed you, keep you as comfortable as possible, and keep you company until the change. When you fully transform under the light of the full moon is when I will extinguish the loup-garou," Logan explained.

Logan grabbed the bottle of liquid, that George began to assume was holy water, and sprinkled its contents on the gun and the bullets. He said a prayer in French and blessed the instruments before he began loading the bullets into the magazine.

George watched the ritual and saw from the light penetrating the barn that it was getting close to sunset. He banged his hands on the iron bars and shouted, "Logan, please don't do this! You have to know that this is not real! Let me go, let me go right now, the cops don't have to know! I won't tell anyone about you!"

"George, I already told you that this is real. I am not delusional. It is going to happen tonight," Logan responded calmly.

"I wasn't bit by anything that night, Logan! Please believe me!" George pleaded.

"I saw what I saw, George. I'm sorry. You haven't noticed any changes in your behavior since that night?" Logan asked.

"No. What changes, Logan?" he replied.

"Nightmares. Nightmares with creatures and yellow eyes, sleep walking, increased appetite, growing aggression, improved and heightened senses, immeasurable strength, increased speed and agility, extreme allergic reaction to silver, and animals responding in fear toward you," Logan said, listing the symptoms of the infection.

George heard Logan's words and only one thought came to mind: Austyn. Logan had perfectly described everything that Austyn had been through since Slaughter Creek. Could what he was saying be true? Thoughts of Austyn's wound healing in a matter of hours, his reaction to a little nick by the silver-plated letter opener, his increased speed, his nightmares, the yellow eyes that Austyn described, the reaction of animals to him.

George sighed heavily. "I am not who you are looking for."

CHAPTER ELEVEN: ON THE LOOKOUT

Austyn sat in his car going over everything that had just happened. His best friend had been taken by a strange man in a black van. There was nothing he could do now except watch the scene play over and over in his mind while he waited for the deputy to arrive. He looked at his phone with tears in his eyes and hesitated calling Damaris. He didn't know how to explain what had just happened, and he knew that George's parents were going to be devastated. He unlocked his phone and selected D's contact info; it rang twice and then she answered.

"Hello Austyn!" D answered happily.

"D…Da…Damaris," Austyn could barely get any words out.

"Austyn what's wrong?" D asked worriedly. She could hear the tears in his voice.

"Damaris, he took George. The man in the black van took George," Austyn blurted out.

"WHAT?! What do mean the man in the black van took George?!" D said in confusion.

Austyn explained to Damaris what had occurred and told her that he was waiting for the deputy to arrive to take the report. After he hung up with Damaris, Austyn returned to the gas station and gas pump where it all took place. He thought that the man in the black van had been a figment of his imagination.

The deputy arrived on the scene and located Austyn. "Hello, I'm Deputy Owens. Are you Austyn Silver?"

"Yes, sir," Austyn replied, wiping his tears .

"Tell me what happened," said Deputy Owens. Austyn gave his account of what had taken place and Deputy Owens noted everything down. When Austyn finished his explanation, Deputy Owens asked, "Were you able to get the license plate?"

"No," Austyn responded sadly.

"About what time did this happen?"

Austyn looked at his cell phone to see the time that he had dialed 9-1-1, and said, "It happened about 9:40 PM."

The deputy noted the time then asked, "What did the suspect look like? Why would anyone want to kidnap your friend?" Austyn described the stranger dressed in black but had no idea why anyone would want to abduct George. The deputy clicked his pen and put it and the notepad away in his shirt pocket, and said, "I'll be right back." Deputy Owens walked to the gas station and spoke with the shift manager.

He asked for permission to review the camera footage to see if the abduction had happened within view of the security camera. The shift manager obliged and took the deputy to the back office where the DVR was housed. Reviewing the camera positioning, they were able to identify three different camera angles that had likely captured everything.

When he reviewed the footage, Deputy Owens saw the red Firebird pulling in, and Austyn going inside to use the restroom. Then the footage on all three cameras was scrambled. A distorted object —most likely the van —could be seen pulling up to the adjacent pump, but the distortion on the cameras became worse and anything that may have taken place after the van's arrival could not be seen. The footage cleared in time to catch Austyn running out of the gas station and driving in the direction of the distorted object.

Deputy Owens and the shift manager were befuddled by the sudden interference with the camera system. They watched the footage two more times, and each time the result was the same. Deputy Owens thanked the manager and went back to the gas pump to inform Austyn of his findings.

When the deputy exited the gas station building, he saw that Austyn had been joined by three others. When they noticed the deputy approaching, Letty stepped away from her husband and wiped her eyes.

"Deputy, please tell me you found something," George Sr. asked in as calm a tone as he could manage.

"I assume you are the family of George Bala?" the deputy asked.

"Yes, I am his mother," Letty said as she stepped forward, tears filling her eyes once more. "Please tell me you discovered something!"

"I reviewed the gas station cameras, and I'm sorry, but the camera system seemed to have gone down during the time of the incident," Deputy Owens explained.

His news was not what the family had wanted to hear. Letty let out a loud cry for her son and fell to the ground holding herself.

D could no longer hold in her tears. She broke down and clutched on to Austyn. With her watery eyes she said, "Where is my brother, Austyn? Why did they take him?"

Austyn had no explanation for what had transpired. He felt that it was his fault that this had happened. Maybe if he would have told George about the strange feeling he had of being followed or about seeing the black van following them, none of this would have happened.

After being released from the scene by Deputy Owens, Austyn and the grief-stricken Balas left the gas station. Austyn and D decided to drive around the city looking for the black van that Austyn had become all too familiar with.

They drove all night and didn't find anything. When morning came, Austyn took D home so she could get some sleep. Austyn told her he was going to do the same, but he knew he couldn't sleep. He wasn't tired; he had to keep going, keep trying to find George. He knew from talks with his father when he was young that seemingly random abductions and kidnappings are commonly unsolved if the person is not found within the first forty-eight hours.

Austyn was driving on the Loop 1604 Highway in the eastern part of the county when he received a phone call. It was his dad's close friend, and current homicide detective with Bexar County. A seed of hope flared in Austyn's heart, and he quickly answered the phone.

"Hello, Detective Ordonez. Please tell me you have some news," Austyn said.

"Austyn, I just found something out. It might be nothing, but at least eight different callers have claimed to have seen a black van with a white male driver with long, dark hair. They all saw this van on the far west side of the county. We have deputies on the West Patrol heavily staffed today and at the top of their bulletin board is that mysterious black van."

"Thank you for the information, Detective," Austyn said gratefully, a small smile coming to his face at the drop of optimism he felt with the news.

"Austyn, I loved your dad like a brother, and I know that's how you feel about your friend. I am providing this information as a representation of what you and your family mean to me. You did not hear anything from me, and please don't get involved. Let us do our job. We are doing our very best. Stay at home and get some rest," Detective Ordonez suggested sincerely.

"Thank you, sir. I appreciate everything," Austyn replied with a lump in his throat. After he ended the call, Austyn looked at the time on his car radio and saw that it was 4:49 PM. It was the time of the year when the sun started setting early. He punched the gas pedal and the Firebird screamed down the 1604 highway heading west.

CHAPTER TWELVE: CURSE OF THE MOON

Back at the abandoned barn, George was being held in his cage by Logan, the self-proclaimed werewolf hunter and part of the shadow operation known as the Guard of Notre Dame. Logan was steadfast in his belief that George would transform into a werewolf under the light of a full moon. There was no doubt in his mind that George was the person he saw being bitten by the last loup-garou that he had cleansed.

Because of the conviction with which he spoke, George was finding himself coming to believe some of what Logan was saying. Logan knew a great deal about what happened that night at Slaughter Creek, and he was able to go into great detail about pretty much everything that Austyn was going through. Then George would think better of it; Logan's claims of the supernatural and of men changing into animals were illogical and impossible.

"Logan, I told you that you've got the wrong person. I don't know who you are looking for, but it isn't me," George said, trying to reason with the man keeping him caged. He refused to say a word about Austyn; he wanted to get out and warn his friend before anything worse happened to him.

"You know, George, I am being quite humane and compassionate by handling your case in the manner in which I am. Once you turn —and you will turn —I will end your curse," Logan said.

"I am not going to turn, Logan. This isn't a movie; you know that, right? People don't turn into werewolves or vampires or anything like that, those are myths," George replied sarcastically before turning away from Logan.

Logan walked away from the cage and back to the table he had set up for the ritual of blessing the instruments he planned on using for executing George when he turned to his werewolf form. He kneeled down and reached into the duffel bag of weaponry and pulled out the smart tablet. He placed a tripod in front of the iron cell, beyond arm's reach of George, and fastened the tablet onto it. He opened a video file titled "Loup-garou Versailles" and footage of a young man in an iron cell similar to the one George found himself in began to play. Logan called out to George, "You will understand once you see this."

George turned around and approached the cage wall where the video was playing. He saw the man circling the cage angrily. The man was yelling in French and then Logan and another man dressed in black walked into the frame.

"That is my brother Anton. This was our last successful hunt together," Logan said. George cast his eyes on Logan then moved them back to the screen of the tablet. The man in the cage suddenly dropped to his knees and began screaming in pain, and George couldn't believe what he saw next.

The man in the cage began to change. Slowly, he transformed from a man into a giant, hairy, wolf-like being standing on two legs. The beast looked ferocious with its large snout, sharp teeth, dagger-like claws, and glowing yellow eyes. The creature charged the cage and hit it with such force that the camera, mounted somewhere at a distance from the cage, shook. Logan and Anton drew pistols and fired at the beast, dropping it almost instantly. The werewolf fell to the ground with a whimper of pain just as quickly as he had transformed into the beast, he once again took the shape of a human, only now he was dead. Just before the video ended, George saw Logan and Anton take a knee and sign the cross over their hearts.

George fell backwards to the ground. He was overwhelmed with disbelief and fear at what he had just seen. Something that could not exist, something he thought was only ever in movies, was indeed real. *What did this mean? Logan wasn't crazy? Monsters do exist? Austyn might actually be a werewolf?*

"Now do you understand why you are here?" Logan asked wistfully.

"Logan, that is not real. It is some kind of production with special effects,"

George argued. Deep down he knew that what he had just seen was genuine, but he couldn't let himself believe it was true.

"George, the sun has set. Soon, the full moon shall complete the cycle for you," Logan replied.

"Logan. For Christ's sake, haven't you ever been wrong?!" George shouted angrily.

"You see this cage? I constructed this with my bare hands. I knew I had twenty-four days until the next full moon, so after I used your license plate to find out where you lived, I purchased this abandoned property. I have spent the last three and a half weeks preparing for this day. This barn was to be where our two destinies collide. Once I had everything set here, I began to follow you and observe your activities. I noted your routines and prepared a plan to catch you and bring you here. So, to answer your question, I am never wrong. The Vatican will see the footage from tonight's cleansing, and I will be absolved from taking your life," Logan responded solemnly.

The Texas sky was a dark blue hue and there were no clouds in sight, just the luster of the constellations and the incandescence of the full moon. Logan's watch alarm blared, and he looked at the watch face. He took a deep breath and made the sign of the cross over his chest. He loaded the pistol with the magazine which carried fifteen blessed silver bullets. Logan pulled the slide of the pistol back, readying the gun. He looked solemnly at George who had backed up into the furthest corner of the cage and pointed the barrel at him. George fell to his knees and tearfully pleaded with Logan, "You don't have to do this! I'm just a normal guy, with a normal life!"

Logan stood in silence staring at George and waiting for his transformation to take place.

George looked to the sky and said, "Please let my family know that I love them." George's life flashed before his eyes and he was overcome with love for his family. When he rubbed his eyes to wipe away the tears, he accidentally tore one of his contact lenses. He pulled it out of his right eye and said, "Guess I won't be needing you anymore." He flicked it to the ground along with the other contact and closed his eyes.

Logan continued watching George, waiting. For the first time, George was able to see a look of confusion on Logan's face.

Logan reached into a holster on his belt and pulled out a blade. "George come here, let me see your hand," Logan called to George.

"Why?" George asked, standing up from his knees. Logan motioned for George to come to him.

"I need to check something," Logan replied with a look of concern. George shook his head no and refused to get closer to Logan. Logan pulled the pistol up and pointed at George once again and said, "Your hand, now!"

George hesitantly walked to Logan and held out his right hand. Logan grabbed a hold of George's hand and slid the edge of the blade across his palm. George let out a hiss of pain, "Argghhh...ouch! What are you doing?!" George angrily shouted at Logan and stepped away from the cage wall.

"Show me your hand!" Logan commanded loudly. George raised his hand, now dripping blood from the slash that ran almost the entire width of his palm. Logan stared at George's palm and blinked. He ran outside and looked up into the night sky. The full moon hung high in the air illuminating the land.

Logan ran back into the barn and asked George, "Why are you wearing contact lenses? Why hasn't your hand healed? Why haven't you turned?"

"Logan, I told you: I am not a werewolf. I wear contacts because I have 20/50 vision in both eyes, my hand hasn't healed because you *just* cut me. I haven't turned because *I'm not a werewolf.* Let me go. Please," George said, once again pleading with Logan. With Logan's seeming realization of the truth about George, he had finally had a glimpse of hope that Logan might see reason. Suddenly, a blood curdling howl rang through the night air. George and Logan both looked around with angst. George looked to Logan and asked, "What was that?"

"Oh no," Logan breathed. "I have made a costly mistake." Logan stared at George in despair. "If it was not you that night, then who..." Logan trailed off, the events of the past several weeks playing through his mind. The night at Slaughter Creek, Thanksgiving night, the day he followed George to the drive-in, the night before at the gas station. While George was at all these places, these events shared another commonality: the other young man that was with George.

"Who is the friend that you were with at the drive-in and at the gas station yesterday? Was he with you the night you visited Slaughter Creek?" Logan asked with urgency.

"He's my best friend," George answered, saying nothing more. He did not want to put Austyn in danger, but everything that Logan said and what he had shown him did raise enough questions in George's mind to be concerned. "If I tell you his name, you have to promise me that you won't kill him. You have to promise that you will give him the opportunity to prove to you that he is not a monster. The same opportunity that you have given me."

"George, we don't have time for this. The call of the loup-garou has sounded, the first night of bloodshed has begun!" Logan said with frustration.

"You need to give me your word!" George said forcefully.

Logan shook his head. "Yes, my word. If I find your friend in human form, I will give him the opportunity to prove he is not a werewolf."

"Austyn. His name is Austyn Silver. Now let me out," George replied. He said a prayer in his head and asked for forgiveness for giving Logan Austyn's name. Logan pulled George's cell phone from his pant pocket and turned it on.

"Quickly, what contact do you have him saved under?" Logan asked hurriedly.

"It's under Austy," George replied. He watched as Logan called Austyn and put the phone on speaker. There was no answer. Logan hung up and put the phone back in his pocket.

"Now what?" George asked curiously.

"We wait," Logan answered

"Wait? For what?" George asked with a befuddled expression.

"News, sirens, police calls, the morning," Logan listed. He exited the barn and returned a moment later with a police radio scanner. He set it down on the table and turned it on.

CHAPTER THIRTEEN: LOUP GAROU

Austyn had crossed the IH-35 highway, which brought him to the west side of the county. It was 9:17 PM; the sun had set three hours ago. Using the glow of streetlights overhead, Austyn scanned all around him for a black van. As he searched, his cell phone rang. He checked it and saw that D was calling him. He answered with the speaker phone, "Hello Damaris."

"Austyn, where are you?" D asked with concern.

"I'm on the road. Looking for the van," Austyn responded.

"Austyn, come home. Your mother is worried and so are we," D replied, almost begging.

Austyn wanted to say something comforting to her, but he couldn't speak. The light of the full moon shone brightly into his car, obscuring his vision. Austyn's feet pulsated and began to rip out of his shoes, driving the gas pedal down to the floorboard. He was in pain. His entire body felt like it was on fire. He lifted his head and looked at his reflection in the rearview mirror. All he could do was stare as his eyes went from the quiet brown that they normally were to a glowing yellow hue. His face began to elongate, and his teeth grew sharp; his ears morphed into pointy, elf-like ears, and his hair turned into a thick coat of dark fur that quickly covered his entire body. Austyn's shirt and pants had ripped off, no longer able to cover his enlarged torso and legs. Austyn's hands on the steering wheel changed into huge paws with razor-sharp claws.

The Firebird was speeding down the road at over a hundred miles per hour, and when it reached the bend in the road, the car flew off the road and straight into the wooded area lining the roadway. The beast that overtook Austyn had flown through the windshield and landed on the grass-covered ground. The werewolf let out a bone-chilling howl and put its nose to the wind. It disappeared into the woods in a flash.

Damaris was still on the phone. She didn't have a clue as to what had happened. She had heard the car speed up and some strange noises that sounded like ripping and growling and though she yelled for Austyn, he didn't answer her. When she heard the howling, she knew something wasn't right. She hung up the phone and took a few deep breaths to try and calm herself while she tried to figure out what to do. Then it hit her. George, Austyn, and she had installed a family app on their phones that allowed them to use their phone's GPSs to locate one another. D did not want to worry her parents more than they already were so she quietly opened the app and set out to Austyn's location.

* * *

On a neatly kept ranch, with a tidily trimmed lawn, enclosed by a six-foot iron privacy fence, Professor Rene Morales's truck was parked in the driveway. The land was home to two cows, a dog, a handful of hens, and one rooster.

Rene was sitting on his living room recliner watching TV. It had been a long day. The students had a way of irritating him. He had graded their tests over the holiday weekend and expected perfect class attendance for the day but he had been missing two students in his honors Calculus class, George Bala and Austyn Silver. He sighed and turned up the news just as an alert ran across the bottom of the screen. It was asking the public to keep an eye out for a nineteen-year-old male that had been abducted by someone driving a black van.

"These kids, always playing around. This is what happens when these idiots drink and do drugs!" Rene complained to the TV.

"What was that, dear?" Rene's wife Rosie asked from the kitchen.

"Nothing, Rosie, just these dang kids. Always getting in trouble and wanting someone else to bail them out," Rene added to his complaints.

"Rene, calm down. You are going to upset yourself and raise your blood pressure," Rosie said sternly to her husband.

"Okay. I'm calm," Rene grumbled, switching the channel to the Monday night football game between Green Bay and Dallas. Unfortunately, the game didn't help Rene's mood, Green Bay was losing by twenty-four points in the second quarter and their quarterback was injured and was going to miss the rest of the season.

"You gotta be kidding me!" Rene yelled at the TV.

"Rene Morales, you calm down right now!" Rosie shouted. Rene mumbled under his breath and ignored messages he was getting from his friend Javi with memes of the Green Bay quarterback in an ambulance.

Rosie rolled her eyes at her husband as she finished washing the dishes from dinner. As she was lost in her task, she suddenly heard a commotion coming from the yard. The cows and the hens were making all sorts of noise, but she couldn't see what was happening. She called back to the living room where Rene was sitting. "Rene, I think the coyotes are back."

Rene looked towards the back door with his glasses hanging down at the end of his nose. He got up and grabbed his flashlight and handgun from his room's nightstand. He mumbled under his breath *"Rene, the coyotes are back!"*, mocking his wife. *You know I'm watching the game...damnit, I can never do what I want,* he complained to himself.

It was dark and chilly outside, and Rene regretted having stepped out in just his boxers and white tank top. With a shiver, he stepped out onto the porch and looked around. He could see every breath he took forming a cloud of air pluming in front of his face. He could hear the ruckus coming from around the corner, so he turned and raised the light, shining it on a buck laying on its side. The animal was being tugged violently leading Rene to think a pack of coyotes was tearing into the deer.

He raised his pistol and shouted, "Hyah, get out of here!" At his words, the buck stopped moving, and the head of a beast that he had never before seen rose from the other side of the carcass. Rene gasped. The beast stood up on its hind legs. Rene was frozen in place. The werewolf growled aggressively and lunged at Rene.

Rene turned and ran back towards his house, then he remembered that he already had his gun in hand. He turned around to see the beast right on his trail. He stopped before the porch steps and raised his gun, pointed at the quickly closing monster, and shouted, "Not today, Satan!" He squeezed the trigger and the recoil from the gun knocked him back. He tripped over the first step of the patio steps and lost grip of his gun. The gun spun in the air and landed on a step behind him. The impact caused the gun to fire and the round struck Rene on his backside. He fell to the ground in a heap of pain and fear. Rene knew his life was over and he couldn't stop the tears coming to his eyes.

Rosie, waiting inside for Rene to return, heard the gun shots and assumed Rene shot at the coyotes to run them off. When he didn't come back inside, she went to go check on her husband. Opening the back door, she found Rene in tears, his eyes closed, holding his bleeding behind with his left hand. In shock, she dropped to her knees.

"Rene, what did you do to yourself this time?! I told you to take those gun classes!" Rosie said angrily as she dialed 9-1-1.

"It was a bigfoot, Rosie! Sasquatch is here in San Antonio!" Rene said hysterically.

"Bigfoot shot you?" Rosie replied sarcastically.

"No, I shot myself. But Bigfoot was chasing me," Rene responded with an expression of pain.

"Why did you shoot yourself?!" Rosie said and started lecturing Rene on the importance of gun safety. Rene eventually passed out from the excruciating pain in his butt and the lecturing from his upset wife.

Several properties west of the Morales land, a couple was enjoying the peace of the night on their back patio with their golden retriever.

The sound of a branch snapping drew the attention of the family dog. His ears stood up and he stared pointedly into the darkness before running to the edge of the yard, barking into the trees.

"Dakota! What is it?" the man asked his concerned dog.

"Luke, what's wrong with Dakota?" his wife asked.

"I'm not sure, Allie. He only acts like this with snakes and coyotes. He probably knows something is out there," Luke replied. Luke motioned with his arm for Allie to stay back, and he got up and approached Dakota. Dakota was standing in an attack position, Luke grabbed Dakota's collar and peered into the darkness of the trees.

"Who's there?" Luke called into the dark beyond the tree. After no response, he pulled on Dakota's collar and guided him back to the patio. Luke faced Allie and threw his hands in the air and said, "Can't see anything."

Luke continued walking and he saw a look of terror on Allie's face, and she yelled, "LUKE!" Luke turned around and saw a pouncing dark beast in midair heading straight for him. Luke was slammed to the ground with violent force. Dakota attacked the beast but was thrown aside with ease. Allie ran inside to get their shotgun. With her hands trembling, she loaded the shotgun and ran back to the patio. She saw Luke laying on the ground covered in blood.

"No, no, no, no, no, no, no," Allie kept repeating as she ran to Luke. His throat was ripped out and his chest was torn open.

Allie called 9-1-1 and could barely get a word out because of her panic and grief.

"My husband...he's dead," Allie cried hysterically into the phone.

"Ma'am what happened to your husband?" the operator on the phone asked.

"He was atta...AHHHHH!!!" Allie screamed in terror as she was now face to face with the beast the killed Luke. The beast put its mouth around her throat and plunged its claws through her stomach. Allie fell lifeless to the ground next to Luke. The werewolf removed his face from devouring Luke's carcass and howled into the sky.

* * *

Away from the property of the gruesome attacks, D was in her plum-colored SUV in search of Austyn. She was already on the 1604 Highway heading west. The signal showed Austyn had stopped along a curve of the highway, but the map showed nothing there that would give a reason for anyone to stop. She was getting close to Austyn's signal. She approached the poorly-lit bend in the road where the Firebird had gone off course. D pulled off onto the shoulder of the road and checked her phone to make sure she had the right location. The app clearly showed Austyn's phone in the same area. She saw red and blue emergency lights in her rearview mirror, speeding down the highway, sirens blaring. A firetruck, two deputy patrols, and an ambulance all blew by her, causing her SUV to sway slightly.

D started her car again and got back on the highway and as she passed the bend in the road, she noticed that the location app was now showing she had moved past Austyn's location. She pulled over to the shoulder once again and placed her hazard lights on. She stepped out of the vehicle and walked using her phone's flashlight to the place her GPS said Austyn's phone was. She saw that there was a drop off at the bend of the road. She shone the light from her phone into the dark dip and was able to make out what appeared to be taillights. Carefully, she made her way down the slope and as she got closer, she heard Austyn's phone ringing. It was the ringtone that he had set specifically for George.

D saw the wreckage of the car and the hole in the windshield. She was horrified at the scene. She nervously looked around and saw Austyn's clothes scattered nearby, ripped up and surrounded by a thick black clump of fur. She peered into the wrecked car and upon seeing Austyn's phone, she grabbed it.

* * *

At the abandoned barn, Logan was listening to the radio and watching the news, looking for any indication of chaos or reports of a strange creature. George had continued to plead with Logan to let him go, but Logan was not planning on releasing George until he was able to complete his mission. A familiar song rang from Logan's pants, George jumped up and said, "Logan, it's Austyn. That's his ringtone!"

Logan pulled the ringing phone from his pocket and saw that the incoming call was labelled as coming from Austy.

"Austyn," Logan said over phone with his heavy accent.

"Who's this?! Where's my brother?!" Damaris shouted at Logan over the phone.

Logan looked to George and said, "I believe it's your sister."

George, with tears in his eyes, replied, "D must be with Austyn. The full moon is out. Everything must be okay."

"D, is it? Are you with Austyn?" Logan asked over the phone.

"Who are you?! What have you done to my brother?! If you hurt him, I'll kill you!" D replied angrily.

"I have George, he is fine. Where is Austyn?" Logan asked again. Logan looked at George. "Tell her that you are okay."

"Logan, why should I help you?! You are deranged! You have me trapped in here like a prisoner!" George responded.

"George, I don't know what else I have to do to prove that your friend is dangerous and that your sister, out in the open as I presume her to be, is in grave danger," Logan said frustratedly.

George was angry at Logan and no desire to help the man, but he still couldn't deny everything that he had been shown and all that Logan had told him.

Logan again spoke to George, "If you love your sister, tell her you are okay. Please." George begrudgingly agreed.

"I'm here, sis, I'm fine. Please answer his questions," George shouted from the cage.

When D heard her brother's voice, a sense of relief washed over her. "What do you want?" D asked Logan.

"Where Is Austyn?" Logan asked one more time.

"I don't know, I can't find him," D answered.

"Listen very carefully, do not call the police. They will not find me or your brother. If you do as I ask, George will be fine, I assure you," Logan replied.

"Your assurances mean nothing to me, you bastard. What else do you want?" D retorted angrily.

"Why do you have his phone? Were you with him earlier?" Logan inquired.

"I haven't seen Austyn since early this morning. He has been out all night and all day today looking for George. I was on a phone call with him when something happened and the connection was lost. I tracked his position with our locator app. I found his car crashed into a ditch on the side of the highway. I heard his phone ringing when you called. His car is here, but I don't know where he is," D explained.

"When did your phone call cut off? Did you find anything unusual at the wreckage?" Logan questioned.

"I mean, his car is totaled. The windshield has a gaping hole in it. It looks like his clothes were ripped."

"Did you find any fur?" Logan asked.

"Yes. How did you know that?" D responded curiously.

Just then, the police scanner sounded as it picked up communication referring to an accidental shooting. Logan said nothing more to D as he listened to the officer on the radio report on the situation.

"3-David-32," the deputy called into dispatch.

"Go ahead, 3-David-32," the dispatcher responded.

"We're good over here. Male subject Rene Morales will be transported to the ER by Medic 6. He accidentally shot himself when he lost his balance and dropped his gun. He is claiming that bigfoot was chasing him," the deputy reported.

"I'm clear, subject claimed bigfoot chased him and he shot himself when he dropped his gun," the dispatcher repeated.

"Ten-four, we will be en route to assist with the animal attack at 1-0-2-4-7 West Forrest Road," the deputy added.

"I'm clear. I'll show you en route to 1-0-2-4-7 West Forrest Road," the dispatcher confirmed and ended the communication.

Logan typed the address into his phone's GPS and asked D, "What is your current location?"

"I am on the 18000 block of Loop 1604," D replied. Logan entered D's position as well.

"You are less than seven miles from the location of an animal attack. Get in your car and meet me in the parking lot of Texas Burger, it is only twelve blocks from you. Do not call the police or tell anyone," Logan replied and hung up the phone.

"What are you going to do to my sister?!" George shouted at Logan.

"I am going to protect her," Logan replied and exited the barn. He returned with zip ties in his hand. He commanded George to turn around. "Walk backwards and bring your hands to me."

George turned around and walked backwards towards Logan, with his hands behind his back. Logan clenched on and tied them together with the zip ties.

"I'm going to unlock the cage. You are coming with me, but don't try to do anything stupid or I will put you to sleep again," said Logan.

"Alright, I promise. Let me out," George agreed. Logan opened the cage door and George stepped out. Logan grabbed him by the arm and walked him to the van.

CHAPTER FOURTEEN: WOLFSBANE

D was parked in the Texas Burger parking lot waiting for the mysterious black van to appear. As much as she wanted to call her mom, she did not tell anyone about her conversation with her brother's abductor, because she did not want to put his life in danger. She watched as the black van turned into the parking lot and pulled up next to her.

The driver rolled his window down. "Get in."

"Where's my brother?" D asked. The driver motioned behind him, signaling for George to say something.

"I'm here, sis," George said.

"Okay, I'm coming," D replied and got out of her vehicle. She walked around to the passenger side of the van and got in. The driver reversed the van, and they left the premises. D was apprehensive about the whole situation; she looked into the back and saw George sitting in the seat with his hands behind his back.

"Thank God you're okay!" D said happily.

"I love you too, sis," George said tearfully.

"Okay, enough," Logan interrupted. "I need you to show me where Austyn's car is."

"Do what Logan says, D," George said to his sister.

"Logan? Fine, but what do you want with Austyn?" D asked Logan.

"I will show you. Please, where is his car?" Logan said as he handed D the smart tablet. D told Logan how to get to the stretch of the road where she had found Austyn's car, and she looked at the tablet he had given to her.

"Hit play, sis. You're not going to believe what this all about. I still don't believe it myself. If you see it too, maybe I won't think I'm crazy," George said.

D gave her brother a puzzled look and then looked at Logan who nodded his head in agreement for her to press play. When she did, she saw footage that made the blood drain from her face, turning her pale with fear and disbelief. She covered her mouth with her hand and watched as the beast was put down.

D turned to her brother and said, "This can't be real."

"I don't know, sis. After hearing Logan's story, seeing that video, all of Austyn's symptoms, tonight's full moon, Austyn's Firebird wrecked with him nowhere to be found, and now it sounds like two attacks by an unknown creature within seven miles of his car? I really think we need to find Austyn," George replied worriedly.

"Finally, you are starting to come around. Please cut those off of your brother." Logan handed D a knife. D looked at the knife and for a split second the thought of stabbing Logan ran through her mind. She was still very unsure about this whole situation. Her brother's abductor was right in front of her, and he had shown her something that went against everything that she had ever known to be true. D turned to her brother again and cut his restraints.

"Oh, thank God!" George said as he rubbed his wrists where the zip ties had rested. As he continued to massage his sore wrists, the police scanner transmitted an update from the animal attack call.

"5-David-31," the deputy called in.

"Go ahead," responded the dispatcher.

"M.E. requested, times two, scene is secured. Looks like possibly a very large and dangerous animal in the area. Start me a supervisor this way, please."

"Ten-four, 5-David-31, M.E. en route times two, scene is secured Night supervisor is also en route," the dispatcher affirmed the transmission.

Logan sighed. "It is too late; your friend has tasted flesh. He will not stop now," Logan said sternly to George and D.

"Logan, you gave me your word," George reminded Logan as he slowed the van to a stop.

"Right down there," D said to Logan before he could answer George's plea. Logan looked to where D's finger was pointing and nodded, and all three of them got out of the van and walked down the slope to Austyn's car.

George was beginning to think that Logan was right about Austyn. With an accident scene like this and how badly wrecked the Firebird was, Austyn should be dead. No one could survive that, yet he was nowhere to be found, only his torn clothing and tufts of fur were on the scene.

George had seen a lot of horror movies; in particular, he had seen plenty of werewolf movies because his dad loved them. But nothing in the werewolf lore of any of those movies ever talked about a cure.

"Logan, is there no cure for this curse?" George asked, looking to Logan who was crouched down looking at the imprints in the grass that led to the woods.

"No. I'm sorry," Logan said empathetically. He stood up and looked at the siblings and said, "I am not going to ask any more of you. You are free to go, all I request is that you do not report me to the police until I purge the loup-garou from your city."

"Logan, Austyn is a brother to me. Please let me go with you, I need to see for myself. I won't tell anyone about you, just take me with you," George pleaded with Logan.

"Me too," D added firmly. "This is crazy, and our parents are probably having heart attacks right now, but Austyn is family, we need to be there."

"Very well, but when the time comes, you must stay out of my way. This infection can spread rather quickly if not dealt with swiftly," Logan replied. Logan felt empathy for George and D. He could see how much they loved Austyn. It reminded him of his brother Anton. His older brother had always taken care of him, and it was on nights like these that he found himself missing him terribly.

A throaty, deep, menacing howl suddenly rang out in the air. Logan looked around trying to determine the direction and distance of the wolf's call. "We need to go!"

As the three drove away from Austyn's car, Logan recited the story of the

Beast of Gevaudan to Damaris and told her of the Guard of Notre Dame, his family's legacy, his brother's death, and the missing pieces from the night at Slaughter Creek.

D could only blink in wonderment at this man. It was a lot to take in, and it all seemed so fantastical that she felt as if she were a character in a horror story. It couldn't be true. She was sure it couldn't. But what if it was? D thought of Austyn and how sweet he was to her, how he knew exactly what to say to cheer her up when she was down, and how much she enjoyed when he was around. She teared up thinking of the possibility that he wouldn't be a part of their lives, of *her* life, anymore.

The van turned onto the property with the abandoned barn and came to a stop. There was no more news on the police scanners or the radio of any sightings of a strange creature or any other animal attacks.

"So, what are we going to do?" D asked worriedly, eyeing the huge iron cage that sat in the barn.

"Unfortunately, we wait. If no more news breaks before dawn, we will have to find Austyn in human form and bring him back here," Logan replied.

"How do we find him?" George asked.

"I'm hoping he finds you," Logan replied before turning to D. "Before you lost contact with him, he was searching for George, correct?" he asked D.

"Yes, but what if he was hurt in the wreck yesterday and taken to the hospital, and everything else that happened last night was purely coincidental?" D added, trying to be rational about an irrational situation.

"Check the hospitals for someone matching Austyn's description then, but don't get your hopes up," Logan replied, checking his watch. It was an hour until sunrise.

"Then what?" D asked impatiently.

"You both will need to get some rest. When he transforms back to his human form, he will be tired. His energy will be drained, and he will sleep for a few hours. When he wakes up, he will think that what he remembers are actually extremely vivid nightmares. He will be dazed, confused, and naked," Logan explained.

"Logan. I have a question," said George.

"What is it?" Logan responded.

"You said it took you five silver bullets to stop this Delacroix guy. It only took you one to put down the werewolf in the video you showed me. Why?" George asked.

"Delacroix was unique. We had never encountered anything like him. He had become aware of his curse and he unleashed it on the public without remorse. Once he learned that he could spread his curse with a bite, he purposely sought out physically strong, but mentally weak individuals so he could control them. I do not know how he did it, but it appeared as though he had learned to maintain control of himself while in the form of the beast. It could very well be the result of the hundreds of years of evolution that the curse has been passed along. Delacroix was the first loup-garou that I have ever had to expend more than one silver bullet to put down. His will was unmatched," Logan replied with regret.

George stood in silence as he processed Logan's response. Meanwhile, D was texting her parents that she was safe, and she and Austyn were searching for George together. She did not want them to worry about her, but she couldn't tell them that she had already found George. They would insist she bring her brother home where they knew he was safe.

George's hand was still bleeding a little bit from the gash that Logan had used to test George to see if he was the werewolf. He washed it off with a bottle of water Logan gave him and tore off a shirt sleeve to wrap around it.

"Why did you cut him?" D asked with an irritated tone.

"It was a test. I had to see if George was the loup-garou," Logan replied. Logan saw a look of exhaustion on George's and D's faces and said, "Look, if you are going to help me find your friend, I need you to get some rest. Charge your phones over there and make sure your ringers are on. When he wakes he will call you, Damaris."

George grabbed a couple of blankets that Logan had sitting on a pile of hay. He passed one to his sister and the two went into a horse stall and laid down for a nap. Logan stayed awake monitoring the police scanner, social media, and local news for any developing stories involving strange creatures or vicious animal attacks.

* * *

The sun rose in the eastern horizon, greeting a crisp, cool morning. An Atascosa County farmland property was busy with activity. The lady of the house, armed with an empty handbasket, walked into the chicken coup to gather eggs for the morning breakfast. When she entered, the coup was in disarray, and the hens were flustered; they charged out of the coup, cooing and clucking once the door opened. To her surprise, she saw an athletic-looking young man laying naked and asleep on the floor of the chicken coup. Egg-gathering forgotten, she ran out of the coup screaming, "Harry! Harry! Oh my God!"

Ten minutes later, Austyn was woken up by the persistent poking of a police officer's baton. When he opened his eyes, he saw two deputies standing over him, doing their best to keep the chuckling to a minimum.

"Wake up, sleepy head!" the first deputy said.

"Looks like someone had a fun night last night," the second deputy observed.

"Where am I?" Austyn said, still groggy from his slumber.

"You are inside of a hen house, and you are naked, son," the first deputy replied. Austyn looked at himself and, with embarrassment, covered up his private areas as much as he could.

"Here," the second deputy said, tossing Austyn a blanket. "Mrs. Anderson was kind enough to let you use this, cover yourself and stand up."

Austyn snatched the blanket and wrapped himself up as he got to his feet.

"I'm Deputy Smith with Atascosa County. What is your name, son?" Deputy Smith asked.

"Austyn. Austyn Silver, sir," Austyn answered, shielding his eyes from the beams of sunlight flowing through the chicken wire.

"Well, Austyn, what we have here is a case of indecent exposure and potentially burglary, but these nice folks just want you off of their property," Deputy Smith explained. "Put your hands behind your back."

"Deputy Smith, I don't even know how I got here," Austyn responded.

"It's okay, Austyn. We can figure this out at the holding cells," Deputy Smith assured him.

Austyn was confused and did not want to make things difficult on the deputies. He turned around and handcuffs were placed on him. He was escorted to the Deputy's patrol vehicle and taken to the Atascosa holding cells.

"Deputy Smith, what is going to happen to me, sir?" Austyn asked shamefully. He had no clue how he ended up naked on someone's property in Atascosa County, and inside of a hen house no less. He remembered driving, looking everywhere he could think of for George, and then everything was a blur.

"Look Austyn, I don't know what you were on last night, but I hope you reconsider putting that trash in your body. You seem to be a good kid; your record is clean, and you are very respectful. The Andersons didn't want to press charges, but you are going to be placed in a holding cell until you can get someone to bring you clothes and pick you up," Deputy Smith replied.

Austyn breathed a sigh of relief and said, "Thank you," under his breath.

Once they made it to the holding cells, Deputy Smith escorted Austyn into a vacant cell where he walked to the bench and sat down. He was trying to figure out what had happened the night before. Flashes of chasing a deer entered his mind, but nothing was coherent. *Where the hell is my car?* He wondered.

"Deputy Smith, sir, when will I be able to make that phone call?" Austyn politely asked the deputy.

"As soon as I get you processed with fingerprints and contact info. Just a formality, due to holding you here. It won't take too long," Deputy Smith answered.

* * *

Back at the barn, Logan, who was snacking on chips and drinking a bottle of water, was still monitoring all local news outlets and social media for anything that could indicate where Austyn was last seen. A ringtone sounded from where George and D were sleeping. It woke the siblings and D ran to her phone. It was a number that she did not recognize.

"Answer it!" Logan ordered.

D answered the phone and after hearing the voice on the other end, tears of joy sprung to her eyes.

"Austyn!" D said enthusiastically. "Thank God you're all right!" George and Logan gathered around her eagerly.

"Hi, Damaris! Yes, I'm okay…well for the most part," Austyn replied half-heartedly.

"Where are you, what is this number you are calling me from?" D asked curiously.

"I'm in an Atascosa County holding cell. I need someone to come pick me so they can release me. I didn't want to call my mom," Austyn explained, shame coloring his words.

"Atascosa County?! How did you end up there? What did you do?" D exclaimed.

"It's a long story, I'll tell you when you get here. Any news on George?" Austyn replied.

"Austyn, I have good news. George is fine, he is right here with me. We have been so worried about you!" D said, overcome with joy.

"Really…oh my goodness…let me talk to him!" Austyn said with elation.

"Bro! I'm fine, we have a lot to talk about!" George spoke into the phone, excited to talk to his friend.

"Yes, we do. I am sorry that I wasn't there to protect you, bro. I am so glad you are alive. What happened to that psycho? How did you get away? Is he in jail?" Austyn had so many questions for his friend, his happiness overshadowing the fogginess of the night before.

"I am good, Austy. Like I said, we have a lot to talk about. We are on our way to get you," George replied excitedly.

"Okay, bro, sounds good. Just one more thing I need to ask," Austyn added.

"Sure, name it!" George replied.

"Bring me some clothes. Please," Austyn said with embarrassment. The phone call ended, and George and D embraced in a hug of jollification for Austyn.

"We need to bring him back here," Logan said breaking up the celebration.

George and D had momentarily forgotten the situation they were caught up in.

"Logan, you were wrong about George. You could be wrong about Austyn," D said. Before she could say anymore, the TV interrupted her with breaking news from overnight.

"Late last night, a couple was killed at their home in a savage animal attack. Police reported that the couple was barbecuing in their backyard when their evening was interrupted by a wild animal. Due to the viciousness of the attack, local authorities believe a mountain lion was the culprit."

Logan turned his gaze to D and said, "We need to bring your friend here to prevent any further bloodshed." He grabbed a pouch from his duffel bag and sat it on the table. From the pouch, he took a scoop of a purple powdery substance and mixed it in with a bottle of water.

"What is that?" George asked curiously as he watched the powder disappear into the water.

"This is wolfsbane. Make sure he drinks thinks this," Logan said as he handed the bottle to D.

"What is this going to do to him?" D asked with a look of concern.

"It will make him weak and tired; he will sleep," Logan explained. "If he has not been tainted by the curse of the loup-garou, nothing will happen to him." He took another scoop and mixed it in another bottle of water and drank it completely to prove his point. He threw the bottle on the ground and said, "There do you believe me? It will not harm your friend, but you must bring him back here."

Logan drove D and George to pick up D's vehicle from the Texas Burger parking lot. George and D hopped into D's SUV and as they were leaving the lot, D gave George a look of concern.

"George, this Logan guy kidnapped you, strong-armed me, and now he wants us to bring him Austyn. Don't you think this is wrong?" D asked her brother.

"I don't know, sis. This is all crazy, I thought Logan was psychotic and delusional. But he let me go when he saw that I wasn't a werewolf. I believe him when he says that he will give Austyn the opportunity to prove he is not a werewolf," George replied.

"George, this is Austyn we're talking about!" D snapped.

"Don't you think I know that! I don't need you pointing things out to me! People died last night, D, just like Logan said would happen. Austyn's car is wrecked and he was nowhere to be found. And when we finally heard from him, we find out he's naked in an Atascosa County holding cell. None of this makes sense. Let's just let him drink the damn bottle of water and we will go from there!" George snapped back.

"Okay, fine. But if he drinks that bottle and nothing happens to him, we are going straight to the police," D said firmly.

"Deal. Just drive." George replied.

The SUV continued on the highway towards the county line and in short order, they arrived at the Atascosa County holding cells. They entered the building and were met by Deputy Smith. George handed the clothes he had brought with him to the deputy, and minutes later Austyn walked through the door fully clothed.

"Hey, Austyn?" Deputy Smith said before the trio made it to the exit.

"Yes, sir?" Austyn turned to face the deputy.

"Stay away from the drugs, son," Deputy Smith advised Austyn. Austyn nodded his head and he, George, and D, walked out of the building and immediately shared a long hug. There were no dry eyes. For the first time in a long while, everything felt right.

"Bro, I'm so glad you are okay. How did you get away from that guy?" asked a tearful Austyn as they made it to the SUV.

"It's a long story. Here you're gonna need this." George handed Austyn the wolfsbane-laced bottle of water. Austyn undid the cap and recoiled.

"Smells kinda funky," he said, frowning at the bottle in his hand, "but screw it I'm thirsty." And without hesitation, Austyn gulped down a good portion of the water.

"Drink up, Austy. And, uh, when you're done," George chuckled, "you're going to need to tell us how you ended up *naked* in an Atascosa County holding cell and your car ended up wrecked in a ditch."

"I don't know exactly wh—my car is where?!" Austyn said as he noticed he was wearing clothes from the gym bag that he had in his car.

George and D tried not to laugh, but the moment called for it.

"My poor baby," Austyn sulked, holding his head in distress. But, after a moment, he couldn't help but join in with D's and George's laughter. He was happy that they were all safe and together again. He regained his bearings and explained the craziness of waking up naked in a chicken coup surrounded by deputies. The SUV was abuzz with laughter.

As he continued recounting what he could remember of his night, Austyn began to feel a little light-headed, and he found himself having trouble keeping his eyes open. He grabbed George's shoulder and said, "I'm not feeling well," before he slumped back into the seat in a deep sleep.

George and D were more disappointed than shocked as they watched Austyn in his induced slumber. They had hoped that the wolfsbane wouldn't have an effect on Austyn, and that the whole thing would be over. D knew that she had to take Austyn to Logan, the exact thing she was trying to avoid.

CHAPTER FIFTEEN: THE PLAN

"Austyn, are you okay?" George called out to Austyn from the other side of the cage. It felt strange seeing his best friend in the same situation that he had found himself in just one day earlier.

"He will be out for a while," Logan said to George.

"Logan, let's say for argument's sake that Austyn does change tonight. If the wolfsbane has this effect on him, can't we just inject him with it so he'll sleep through the nights of full moons?" D asked hopefully. She didn't want to believe that there was even the slightest chance that Austyn was a werewolf, but she wanted to have all of her bases covered.

"Wolfsbane was originally used against the loup-garou, when a group of monks were traveling back to their monastery. They were attacked by a loup-garou and two of the monks fell. But Brother Manuel had spent some time earlier that day picking flowers and as he did, one he had never seen before stood out to him. He claimed that God told him to keep it with him and that it would bring him peace. Brother Manuel had picked wolfsbane. He held in his hands when the beast approached him, he put his hands in front of his face for protection and the pollen from the flower spread on the face and fur of the beast. It stopped in its tracks and ran the other way, leaving Brother Manuel untouched." Logan held a single flower in his hand. "The Lord, in his infinite wisdom, placed this magnificent flower on this earth to protect us. But for the benefits that wolfsbane brings, it cannot tame or even kill a loup-garou. It is best used as an irritant and deterrent. If a loup-garou is strong or hungry enough, wolfsbane would only cause him a slight discomfort."

D's hope quickly faded. She was running out of ideas and arguments. She looked to her brother who was sitting next to the cage near where Austyn was sleeping. D prayed that everything would be okay, and that they would all make it home after tonight. She looked at her watch; it was already past 7 PM.

Austyn began to flutter his eyes open. As he got to his feet, feeling extremely dazed and confused, he realized that he was once again in a cell. He saw George and D standing outside of the cage looking at him with concern. He turned his head to the left and saw the mysterious man in black that had kidnapped George. Austyn charged the bars, hitting them with such force that the heavy-duty cage shook.

"Guys, run! This lunatic is back!" Austyn yelled to his friends. But when he turned to look at them, they weren't moving, and the kidnapper moved closer to stand beside them. Austyn's anger turned to confusion. "What's going on?"

"Austyn, this is Logan. Yes, he is the guy that kidnapped me, but he didn't hurt me. Well, aside from cutting my hand, he didn't hurt me," George explained.

"What?!" Austyn exclaimed in utter confusion.

"Austyn, please listen to what Logan has to say. We are trying to help," D pleaded with him.

"Why do y'all have me trapped in this cage?" Austyn asked.

"Austyn, your friends do not want to see you in this cage. But I have shown them some proof that this cage is necessary for our safety and yours," Logan said.

"What the hell are you talking about?! Who the hell are you?!" Austyn asked angrily.

"I am a Logan; I am a hunter of sorts. Part of a long line of defenders of the peace and of the Catholic Church," Logan replied.

"A hunter?! So, what? You hunt people and turn their friends against them?!" Austyn angrily replied.

"No, Austyn Silver. I do not hunt *people*, I hunt *werewolves*," Logan stated calmly.

"Oh, am I a werewolf or something?" Austyn scoffed. "Give me a break." Austyn looked at George and D and noticed the shared look of concern on their faces.

"Where were you last night, Austyn?" Logan asked.

"I…I was…" Austyn tried hard to remember the previous night, but he couldn't. He saw flashes of himself in his Firebird, he saw himself looking into the rearview mirror and seeing a pair of yellow eyes looking back at him, then he saw himself chasing a buck through the woods. They were all broken images that didn't make sense.

"You can't answer because you do not remember. You do not remember because yesterday when the full moon rose, you changed into a loup-garou, a werewolf. You murdered two innocents last night," Logan added.

"What?! No! I didn't! I couldn't have," Austyn answered, worry and fear coloring his voice. Logan held up his smart tablet with the news feed that told the story of the gruesome deaths of the couple in their own backyard on the southwest side of the county.

"I thought George was the werewolf, and that is why I took him. He was in your place last night. When he did not turn, I knew I had made a grave mistake, and now two people are dead, and one is in the hospital," Logan explained.

Austyn stared open-mouthed at Logan.

"It's true, Austyn," George said. "He explained everything to me yesterday and was planning to execute me once I changed under the light of the full moon. He was wrong. He thought I was attacked that night at Slaughter Creek."

"This has to do with Slaughter Creek?!" Austyn was astonished at what he was hearing.

"Yes, Austyn, it was me whom you saw shooting at the creature in the woods that night," Logan replied.

"You killed the naked guy that night?!" Austyn said with anger.

"That naked guy was a werewolf, Austyn; a very strong werewolf that was ready to kill many of you gathered at the creek before making the rest of you like him in an attempt to restore his pack," Logan responded.

Austyn couldn't believe what he was hearing. Aside from feeling a little betrayed and angry, he felt like he was losing his mind. It seemed as if his world had been turned inside out, ever since that night at Slaughter creek. He looked at George and Damaris and said, "How can y'all stand there and let this happen to me?"

"Austyn, I don't believe any of this. But you don't remember anything from last night, and you passed out when you drank the wolfsbane-water." Damaris replied teary eyed.

"Austy, this will be over once the moon is full." George added trying to put his friend at ease.

"Austyn, your friends do not have any ill-intent towards you in this unfortunate situation. They are hoping that I am wrong in my summation, but I cannot afford to let you roam free under the full moon. You will change, and you will kill again." Logan said as he stood in front of the cage, face to face with Austyn.

"This can't be happening!" Austyn said out loud.

"But it is, mon ami. It is," a voice echoed through the barn. Out of the shadowy corner appeared the dead naked Frenchman that Austyn had seen in his nightmares.

"Delacroix!" Logan shouted in surprised horror. He jumped in front of George and D, but when he moved to draw his pistol with the silver bullets, it wasn't on him. His eyes traveled to where it sat on the table and he knew that Delacroix would surely beat him to it if he attempted to grab it.

"Yes, you filth. I, the ultimate alpha, still live," Delacroix announced with a sinister laugh. "The orb of my power is nigh; you will pay for what you did to my family!" Delacroix shouted in rage.

"They were not your family," Logan replied with disdain. " They were innocents that you cursed with your bite. They were a pack of heathens that you controlled like a puppet master."

"It was a gift that I gave them! You took them from me!" Delacroix snarled.

"Does this mean that Austyn isn't a werewolf?" George asked in the middle of the heated conversation.

"Oh no, my boy." Delacroix turned an evil smile to George. "I'm afraid it is true. I gave Austyn my gift, and he gave me an opportunity for something that I greatly desired. Revenge," Delacroix explained.

"What nonsense do you speak of?" Logan snapped.

"Austyn has been a pawn in my master plan since my resurrection," Delacroix said by way of explanation.

"How dare you compare yourself to the almighty! You vile, blasphemous creature!" Logan retorted angrily.

"You were resurrected?" D asked with concern. George, D, and Austyn were mystified by the entire exchange.

Delacroix paced in a circle in front of the barn door and removed his long coat, letting it fall to the floor. He glared at D and said, "Yes. Despite his attempts, Mr. Bergier hadn't killed me that night, but he had fatally wounded me. Because of you idiotic young people, the police were called to the area and Mr. Bergier was not able to finish his job. He had no doubt hoped that he had done enough and assumed the stream would carry me away, believing I was too weak to fight against its current. Unfortunately for him, I made it to solid ground." Delacroix stared at Logan and said, "Where I died." After a tense moment of silence, Delacroix turned his attention back to D and continued. "During my autopsy, the blessed medical examiner determined the cause of my death to be gunshot wounds. When he removed the last of the five silver bullets from my body, as luck would have it, I began to heal. After that, well," Delacroix gave D a malicious grin, "let's just say we exchanged places. I then went out in search of my pup, Austyn there." He nodded at Austyn in the cage. "I knew that Logan would definitely hunt the young man he saw me bite at the creek. To my happy surprise —and much to my enjoyment—you mistakenly took his friend as your prisoner. Last night, under the veil of the full moon, while you were busy with your prisoner, I called to Austyn. He came to me, and I sent him after a deer that was running into someone's property. He caught the deer, but that idiot in his underwear frightened him off with his gunfire. Because Austyn is so young, I realized I had to take things into my own hands, so I made my way to the nearest property that I could smell flesh, and I engorged myself."

"So, Austyn didn't kill anyone?!" D responded.

"Unfortunately, no, but I knew the news of an animal attack would reach Logan and that Logan would see the attack for what it was, would realize he had the wrong man in captivity, and would make it his mission to catch Austyn. I sat in waiting and followed you from the holding center. You have all led me right to my prey. Though he did not devour anyone last night, Austyn will have his first taste of flesh tonight as he rips into you and your brother. Or perhaps, maybe just a bite from me to add you to my new family," Delacroix said to D, licking his lips. In a blink, Delacroix moved from the barn entrance to the cage door. He had taken the gun from Logan's table and shot the lock on the door allowing it to open a crack. Logan's face held a look of despair.

"I don't much like these primitive devices, but on occasion they do come in handy." Delacroix withdrew the magazine loaded with the silver bullets and flung it towards the barn entrance, and he turned and tossed the gun onto the table.

Logan eyed the gun. *I need to get to my weapons,* he thought to himself. He knew he had to come up with a distraction, and fast. Delacroix noticed Logan's eyes flick to the table, and before Logan could develop another thought, Delacroix was standing in front of him, holding him by the throat.

"Tsk, tsk, tsk. None of that now. I want you here in my grip when I turn."

George and D watched in terror as Delacroix lifted Logan in the air with one arm.

"Put him down!" D yelled.

"All In due time, my pretty. Don't worry, there is something grand in store for you and your brother," Delacroix replied. George saw Logan struggling to breathe as he tried to break free of Delacroix's grasp. As he looked around, desperately trying to figure out what he could do, George saw the head of the pouch of wolfsbane poking out of Logan's jacket pocket and he had an idea. He turned to D who was next to him, and Austyn, who was still standing in the unlocked cage. "I need to get that pouch from Logan's pocket," he said as quickly and quietly as he could.

Not wasting a moment, George ran towards Logan, hoping to catch Delacroix off guard, but the man was too quick. He must have seen George running at him and turned in time to grab George by his throat with his free hand. As he lifted him from the ground, George's legs dangled helplessly in the air.

Unexpectedly, D charged at Delacroix and said, "Let him go!" and began pounding on him with her fists. Austyn had already started to run to them when Delacroix flung George to the ground. George slid on his back and was stopped with the thud of his head hitting against the corner post of the cage. Delacroix hit D with his palm knocking her backward with force and said, "Patience my dear. Good things come to those who wait."

Austyn exited the cage and rammed Delacroix from the side; the force of which being enough to move Delacroix from his planted position, but not enough for him to let go of Logan. Delacroix held Austyn's head back with his extended right arm. "Easy my pup," he said. "The aura of the full moon is upon us, et vous êtes le prochain."

D had managed to get back to her feet and, while Delacroix was preoccupied, ran to Logan's left jacket pocket. She reached in pulled out the pouch of wolfsbane. D jammed her hand in the pouch and grabbed some of the powder in her hand. Hurriedly, she moved to Delacroix and rubbed the wolfsbane into his eyes.

Delacroix let out a fearsome groan, releasing both Logan and Austyn, and frantically rubbing his eyes. "You petulant little fool!" he roared. "What have you done!"

Logan regained his footing and ran to his weapons still scattered on the table. Delacroix stumbled after him and swung his arm in Logan's direction, but Logan was able to duck and roll under the swipe. Austyn jumped to his feet and ran to ram Delacroix once more. George had picked up a two-by-four that had been on the ground next to where he landed. He got to his feet, ready to run and attack Delacroix as well, hoping to give Logan enough time to set up his arsenal. But that's when George noticed that Austyn had stopped hard in his tracks and fallen to his knees. Delacroix seemed to have noticed Austyn's behavior as well and ceased struggling. He threw his head back and laughed, blinking his irritated eyes.

"It is too late. The moon is full, and Austyn shall be under my command from this day forward."

CHAPTER SIXTEEN: BLOOD BROTHERS

D and George watched in horror as Austyn transformed into a ferocious beast. A werewolf. The creature that was once Austyn stood on his hind legs and looked to Delacroix as though awaiting instruction.

"Austyn," D whimpered, tears running down her cheeks.

"My brother," George choked out, moving to stand in front of his sister.

The beast was heaving and growling, and in a single bound moved to stand at the side of his master, his alpha. Delacroix appeared to have changed, but only partially. He stood next to Austyn, in the body of a man with very wolfish features and yellow eyes. He petted Austyn and commanded, "Go, my pup." Taste the flesh you so deeply desire."

Werewolf Austyn turned and saw Logan loading his gun, and with a grumbling growl he lunged for him. Logan was only able to grab his silver-plated daggers before he was forced to slide away from Austyn and quickly climb the ladder to the second level of the barn; the gun lay on the ground with a half-loaded magazine next to it.

Delacroix snarled at Austyn. "What are you waiting for?! Get him! Feed!"

Austyn looked to Delacroix and then jumped at the ladder and scrambled up over the edge, letting out a loud howl.

"And as for you two," Delacroix said, turning to George and D. "Just watch for now, but don't worry, we won't forget about you." While he tried to maintain his haughty confidence, Delacroix was struggling to speak. His physical features had slowly begun to change. His ears were pointed, his hands now had claws, and he appeared darker because of slowly emerging fur. Delacroix looked up to the second level and listened attentively. George and D had backed up into a corner, fear plain in their eyes.

"Cuando el viene por me, ve y agarra la pistola que se le callo a Logan," George whispered to D, telling her to grab Logan's gun when Delacroix comes after him.

"What?! I'm not goin —"

George put his hand over her mouth. "Just do it, D! For once, listen to me! Please!" George barked at his sister. D looked at him for a moment before reluctantly nodding her head.

On the second level of the barn, Logan was hiding behind a support beam. He could feel the vibration of the floor every time Austyn took a step or leapt from place to place. When he heard the werewolf sniffing deeply, Logan was more grateful than ever for the specialized chemical he wore that hid his scent from creatures, including the loup-garou.

Austyn got down on all four limbs and was slowly prowling the upper platform of the barn. Logan knew Austyn was close and that he would be found if he didn't make a move. He spotted an open window and determined that to be his only avenue of escape. Breathing deeply to steady himself, he held the daggers in his hands, ready to throw them at his hunter. Quickly, Logan bounced out from behind the beam and made a run for the window. Austyn turned at the sound and charged at him, but right as he was about to swat Logan with his right arm, Logan unleashed the daggers. One dagger struck the left side of Austyn's chest and the other struck his right hand in the same spot that he had stabbed himself with the silver-plated letter opener in George's attic. Austyn groaned in pain and flailed violently, desperate to remove the daggers. Logan flew out of the window, as he was struck by Austyn's flailing arms. He rolled off the roof and landed on top of a bale of hay.

"Hurry and finish the job!" Delacroix yelled in frustration, having seen Logan escape. Austyn, still with his expression of pain, jumped out the window to follow Logan.

Delacroix, his transformation now complete, refocused on George and D, but said nothing. Saliva dripped from his snarling mouth as he stared them down. Suddenly, Delacroix let out a howl at the moon and began moving towards George and D. George grabbed the two-by-four again and looked at D. "Go!" he shouted, and he swung the piece of lumber at Delacroix. The wood connected with the beast and shattered on impact, causing Delacroix to lose his balance and bump George with his forehead, knocking him to the ground.

D ran out from behind the cage when her brother yelled. She grabbed the gun and the magazine off the ground and had never been more grateful for all those times Austyn had taken her and George to the shooting range. With a practiced hand, she inserted the magazine, racked the slide back, and aimed at Delacroix who was now holding George down, teeth bared and ready to bite.

Bang! Bang!

Two gunshots rang out in rapid succession. Delacroix was struck on his leg and in his back. Before D could shoot again, he darted off into the darkness of the barn, growling in anger and pain.

Outside, Logan had hidden himself in surrounding bales of hay while Austyn scanned the area around the barn from the rooftop.

Logan was down to his last dagger and he wasn't sure he would be able to manage much of a fight if Austyn found him. Four of his ribs had broken when Austyn swatted him out the window and he was having trouble breathing. At the sound of gunshots from the barn, Logan knew that he had to get inside. He was the hunter. He had a job to do. He peeked around the bales of hay obscuring him and noticed his van nearby.

Logan burst from behind his hay walls and ran to the van, opening the back doors and quickly digging through his arsenal. He found his brother's pistol and grabbed it and immediately noted that it was not loaded. Logan rummaged around the inside of the van looking for a magazine. His heart fell when he realized that he had placed all his magazines and ammunition into the duffle-bag that was sitting inside of the barn. But then he remembered the magazine that Delacroix had tossed towards the barn entrance. If he was quick, he could reach it before Austyn reached him.

When he had burst from the hay, Austyn spotted Logan from the pitch of the roof. He watched at Logan darted to his van then turned and started moving toward the barn. With a growl, Austyn jumped down to the ground to pursue his quarry. He sprinted towards Logan on all fours and before the man could open the door, Austyn rammed him through the door, completely splintering the lumber. Logan rolled on the barn floor and hit a beam. Austyn stood on his hind legs, shook off the splintered wood, and targeted Logan again.

* * *

Amidst the commotion, D was crouched down beside George. "George, wake up!" D frantically cried, shaking her brother. George winced and slowly opened his eyes. Despite their blurriness, he could see the worry on his sister's face. As his vision cleared, he looked past her at the cage and could make out a large, dark figure standing on top of the cage above his sister. "The cage," was all he could manage to mumble.

D whipped around and saw a salivating Delacroix coming at her from the top of the cage. Though she tried to move, it was too late. Delacroix already had his hands around her shoulders.

George's eyes widened in panic; he had no idea what he could do to help his sister. And then he saw it: the gun laying at Delacroix's feet. He crawled to the weapon as quickly as he could and gripped it tightly. Delacroix looked down and violently kicked George against the wall of the cage before he could get a shot off. D screamed when her brother hit the cage.

"Stop it!" she shouted at Delacroix. Swinging her legs, she kicked Delacroix in the groin. He momentarily flinched and, with a fearsome growl, he grabbed her lower leg, snapping it as though it were nothing more than a brittle twig. She screamed in excruciating pain as her tibia and fibula protruded from her leg. She looked beyond Delacroix with her teary eyes, and saw Austyn about to slay Logan. It was then she did the only thing she could think of; one last attempt to save their lives. "Austyn!" she shouted. "Please... help! Austyn please…aaaahhhhh." But her words were cut off when Delacroix began to squeeze her shoulders, seemingly trying to crush her completely.

Austyn's ears twitched in the direction of D's cry for help, and he stopped his pursuit of Logan. He turned and saw Delacroix holding D; she was crying and in pain. Austyn also saw George laying limp on the ground next to the cage with blood streaming from his mouth.

Delacroix dropped D to the ground and straddled her. He held her head down, exposing her jugular. He opened his mouth of razor-sharp teeth and went in for the bite, but his jaw snapped at air. He was being pulled away from D by his hind legs.

Austyn firmly gripped Delacroix's hind legs and swung him hard against the cage. Delacroix rebounded quickly and got to his feet. He roared angrily and glared at Austyn who was now protecting D and George. Austyn growled and his wolf-like face contorted into an expression of ferocity. He postured aggressively with his arms and claws and lunged at Delacroix, entangling the other werewolf in a furious battle.

Delacroix was much bigger than Austyn and blood soon splattered everywhere as the two lycanthropes gashed, slashed, and gnawed at each other. Delacroix picked up Austyn and slammed him into the ground. While Austyn was on the ground, Delacroix punctured just below Austyn's ribcage with his claws. Austyn let out a whimper as his blood pooled beside his body. Delacroix stood to his full height and looked down at Austyn before swiftly diving down to bite down on Austyn's neck. With his jaw clenched around Austyn's throat, Delacroix intended to choke the life out of him.

"This is for Anton!" Logan declared and opened fire at Delacroix.

Bang, bang, bang, bang, bang!

Logan fired his gun until he heard the telltale *click* of an empty handgun.

Logan's energy was spent. Breathing heavily, he clutched at his midsection, favoring his ribs, and his face was bloodied and bruised. He fell to his knees once again, his strength now completely drained. He tossed the gun to the side and looked up to the heavens.

Every round that Logan had fired struck Delacroix, the majority hitting him on his broad back. The werewolf now lay on the floor, seemingly now dead. Delacroix's body was splayed next to Austyn who was laying still. The only movement coming from him was the slow rise of fall his chest with the slow, deep breaths he was taking.

George, who had regained consciousness, was sitting up, taking in the scene around him, as D sat by his side in shock, staring at her broken leg. To the siblings' horror, Delacroix began to move, making his way up on all fours. Heaving heavy breaths, he scanned the barn. Spotting Logan, he roared and charged directly for him. He pounced on the almost lifeless man and dug into Logan's right leg with his claws. Logan's thigh split open, and Delacroix ripped out a chunk of flesh, prompting a scream of agony from Logan. Delacroix swallowed the meat and moved to Logan's face. Logan looked Delacroix in the eye. The monstrous beast held the stare for a moment before biting down on Logan's throat. But just as he was about to rip out his jugular, Delacroix whimpered in pain. He released Logan's throat and stood up. Logan had driven his last silver-coated dagger into Delacroix's chest. Delacroix ripped the dagger from his chest, and without hesitation stabbed Logan in his stomach. Logan moaned weakly, blood bubbling from his mouth, as Delacroix applied more pressure with his supernatural strength. It took only seconds longer for Logan to stop breathing, his heartbeat ceasing entirely.

The evil beast now turned his attention to the siblings and limped towards them. Before he could get to them, George raised his arm. He was holding Logan's gun and fired every round in the magazine, each strike jolting Delacroix, forcing him, briefly, down on a knee. But once again, he stood up and started towards George and D, single-minded purpose in his eye. The two were anticipating the worst and knew there was no way out. They could no longer defend themselves and Logan was dead. George mustered what strength that he had left and moved his body in front of D in an attempt to protect his sister.

Delacroix's movement abruptly stopped and a groan of pain escaped his lips. Austyn's jaws were clamped tightly around Delacroix's left leg. He then stuck his claws into Delacroix's gut and lifted him off the floor and slammed him against the cage with punishing force. Austyn reached back with his right arm and slashed him across the throat. The once mighty beast fell to his knees, grasping at his throat with both hands as his blood poured from his throat and onto the floor.

As he lay dying, Delacroix slowly changed back to his human form. With his eyes wide open and bulging, he reached for Austyn.

"Tu m'as trahi," he uttered.

Delacroix finally slumped down to the floor, lifeless. The beast had been slain by the creation he once hoped would give him unmatched power.

Austyn looked to his friends and crawled to them. As he crawled, he started changing back into Austyn Silver. He was severely wounded, and bleeding excessively. Austyn's throat had a deep laceration, and his chest had a gaping wound from the silver dagger. When he reached his friends, he fell over on his back, gasping his last breaths.

George removed his shirt and threw it over his friend's lower body. With tears streaming down his face, he looked to his sister. "D, do something! Help him!"

"George, I'm sorry, there's nothing I can do," D said sadly. Even though her medical training wasn't complete, she knew from all the injuries to Austyn's vital organs nothing she did would make a difference.

"Don't worry about…me," Austyn said weakly.

"Austyn, save your strength. We will get help," D said mournfully, trying to comfort Austyn.

"Damaris…if I…I would have…asked you out…" Austyn said through labored breaths.

"Yes…Yes…I would have loved to go out with you!" D said with a tearful giggle. Austyn smiled and weakly pumped his fist.

"Austy…you can't leave me bro," George said grievously to his friend.

Austyn held out his hand to his best friend. George grabbed it and they did their special handshake one last time.

George gave his friend a kiss on the forehead. "I love you too, Austyn. Blood brothers for life."

The Bala siblings sat next to their friend comforting one another as they watched Austyn fade away into the afterlife.

About the Author

Born and raised in San Antonio, Texas, I grew up loving family, baseball, and writing. Werewolves had always intrigued me from the first time I saw one on a TV show as a child. After a mishap occurred 20 years ago, I lost the manuscript for the original book I was writing. I had given up on the dream of becoming an author. I met the love of my life, Letty, and told her about my failed attempt. Through the years our family grew to four, with our children Damaris and George. My wife always encouraged me to start again and finish the book. She has always been my biggest supporter. In 2019, in the midst of the Covid-19 pandemic, I finally caved in and began writing again. This novel has been a dream come true and I am proud that I get to share it with everyone. Don't give up on your dreams, go after them!

Made in the USA
Monee, IL
19 December 2021